CAN I CALL YOU SOLDIER?

CAN I CALL YOU SOLDIER?

DR. HAROLD D. DAVIS

MOODY PUBLISHERS
CHICAGO

All Scripture quotations, unless otherwise indicated, are taken from the King James Version.

Cover Design: Carlton Bruett Design
Cover Image: Stock Illustrations
Editor: Francesca Gray

ISBN: 0-8024-1166-5
ISBN-13: 978-0-8024-1166-2

Library of Congress Cataloging-in-Publication Data

Davis, Harold D.
Can I call you soldier? / Harold D. Davis.
p. cm.
ISBN-13: 978-0-8024-1166-2
1. African American men—Conduct of life. 2. African American fathers—Conduct of life. I. Title.

E185.86.D3865 2006
248.8'42108996073—dc22

2006018141

3 5 7 9 10 8 6 4

Printed in the United States of America

DEDICATION

There are men in every city who have taken it upon themselves to make a difference in the battle to save our boys. Maybe you know one of these men, or possibly you are one of them.

These men neither wait for governmental funding, nor do they need the support or approval of a board of directors. They have the fortitude to stand strong in the face of opposition. They are motivated by the masculine drive to protect and provide for the next generation. They celebrate and nurture their offspring, raising them to be secure and confident.

Our nation and communities will stand or fall on the availability of men who are willing to sacrifice their own pleasure for the sake of others. It is to these men that this book is dedicated. May their tribe increase, for the need is great.

★ ★ ★

CONTENTS

★ ★ ★

The ultimate measure of a man is not where he stands in moments of comfort and convenience, but where he stands at times of challenge and controversy.

DR. MARTIN LUTHER KING JR.

★ ★ ★

INTRODUCTION

This book serves as a wake-up call to all men, specifically black men. Today more than ever, there is a critical need for mature male leadership. Voices from the past like that of Dr. Martin Luther King Jr. beckon this generation of men to be servants who honor the sacrifices that have been made.

I will spare you the pain of negative statistics. Even casual observation gets the point across. Most of us have been touched in some way by the problems of drug abuse, incarceration, and other maladies that are destroying thousands of young black men.

Our current situation warrants an all-out mobilization against these negative forces. Many remedies have been postulated, but I believe that the primary solution rests with the involvement of mature black men. Current research and practical experience support this viewpoint. It is time for men to strategize, organize, and implement solutions.

With this book, I hope to stir your emotions and inspire you to join those who are involved in stemming the tide. It is written to be a first guide, a text of fundamentals, and a primer for how to get engaged. Now is the time for your concern to move to positive action.

★ ★ ★

Can I call you soldier?

★ ★ ★

★ ★ ★

One of the characteristics of a society that is in decline is when the mature men [soldiers] neglect to nurture the next generation of men.

Dr. Harold D. Davis

★ ★ ★

CHAPTER ONE

THE URGENCY OF THE HOUR

It has been said that nobody in this generation will forget where he was or what he was doing on the morning of September 11, 2001. I clearly remember where I was on that dreadful day. The images of the burning towers are still fresh in my mind these many years later.

Various government agencies still point fingers at one another, trying to determine what caused the breakdown in intelligence that allowed this attack to be carried out so efficiently. I believe that a key factor in the success of the enemy was the dullness of the gatekeepers. People in charge of our security had forgotten some important things about the enemy, which made them overlook obvious clues that an attack was imminent. For example, some of the hijackers (from the Middle East) told their flight school instructors that they wanted to learn how to fly and turn large jets but did not seem particularly interested in learning how to land them. That alone should have been enough to alert thinking individuals that something was wrong. And at least one instructor did report his student to the FBI.

That dreadful day, as bad as it was, represents only one type of threat to our nation. There are many different threats that we need to be concerned about. I believe the void that has developed between strong, mature men and the next generation is a considerable threat to the stability of our nation and to the black community in particular. This is the threat that we are addressing in this book.

Consider the following commonsense facts that are being overlooked by much of our culture.

Men Make Men

A boy should learn how to be a man by watching men. I attribute my masculinity to the time I spent with my father. He did not sit me down and say, "This is how you be a man," but he simply lived out his masculinity on a daily basis. I saw him persevere in times of stress and not turn around during difficult times. He dealt with the abuse and prejudice of the day with seasoned wisdom and tact. Because our family did not have a lot of money, his creativity was always in full swing. I realize today that the greatest gift my father gave me was to live before me in a godly, masculine manner. "Train up a child in the way he should go: and when he is old, he will not depart from it" (Proverbs 22:6).

Men Teach Boys How to Love Women

A boy should learn how to treat a woman by watching his father sacrificially love his mother. In today's society many young men have the false notion that marriage is for their pleasure only. Many have not been taught the realities of marriage or seen them demonstrated.

The true richness in marriage comes not on the honeymoon but after many years of facing life's difficulties together. This requires hanging in there through tough times as opposed to quitting like many men do. The apostle Paul told Timothy to "endure hardness, as a good soldier of Jesus Christ" (2 Timothy 2:3). The hardness for most men takes the form of rejecting the desire to be served and becoming your wife's servant. This battle with self is a lifelong challenge.

At the University of Illinois, my wife conducts a choir of over one hundred young people. She is a mother figure to many of the young people, and I am a father figure. On one occasion a young man approached me and said, "Reverend Davis, we enjoy watching you and Sister Davis interacting as husband and wife. We have never seen a couple like you two before." Men who are committed to battle to keep their marriages intact are critically needed for the stability of our nation.

Men Teach Boys How to Persevere

A boy learns how to persevere through difficult times by watching his father and other men persevere. I distinctly remember one occasion when my father came home in the evening only to be greeted by my mother and five hungry children. My mother said to him, "John, we don't have any dinner." Without missing a beat, my father said, "Come on, Bud." He turned and we walked to the west side of town (about three miles), where he asked Mr. Peeples if he could cut his grass because he needed a couple of dollars to feed his family.

Seeing that it was dark, Mr. Peeples protested and tried to give him the money, but my dad refused to take it without working. After he cut the grass (in the dark), he received his pay, and we bought some food and walked home.

I was so affected by that event that it has motivated me in many areas where I wanted to quit. By my father's actions I learned that men of force are actually soldiers who never quit when serving God or family.

Bad Parents Raise Confused Sons

A boy who is raised by a domineering, angry, or addicted parent will have issues to overcome. After many years of counseling, I have come to believe that the majority of problems that we have in our communities and schools find their origins in the home.

A coach recently told me that a boy on his team said to him, "Coach, my daddy is crazy!" The coach told the boy that he should never speak of his father in those terms. The boy then replied, "But coach, you don't understand. My daddy is crazy!" The coach then scolded the boy and told him he didn't ever want to hear that again. Two days later, the boy's father showed up at the first game. The coach saw how he was dressed and how he acted, and after the game he walked up to the young man and said, "Boy, your daddy is crazy!" He had to be honest that this man's behavior was not right nor something his son should copy.

As I interact with children in the public schools, I encounter a disturbing number of boys who have parents who are not prepared to raise them. In previous generations, parents and grandparents raised boys using the Bible as their guide. We all know men who were raised in this manner, and many of them became leaders. Families have changed today, and their boys need help sorting out the issues they face every day.

Absentee Fathers Hurt Sons

A boy who has no father is susceptible to low self-esteem and many other maladies.

I find it very comforting to see a new trend where society is recognizing the harm associated with absent fathers. God's design is that a boy is to jump off into adulthood from the broad shoulders of his father. The tragic injustice is that a vast number of boys are entering their adult years from the ground level.

The list of problems with fatherlessness in America goes on and on. We see the warning signs in our youth culture, where increasing numbers of young men do not understand masculinity. Many are choosing to change their sexual preference with little provocation. We see single mothers struggling to raise sons who are well-balanced. We hear about teens running around with street gangs, getting involved in crime, and joining the exploding prison population.

The Enemy We Are Fighting

The handwriting is on the wall. The Enemy's plan is unfolding as we speak. The various components are in place, and the target is the family. Once the American family is destroyed, the good things about America will be spoken of in the past tense. Traditionally, the band that keeps everything together has been the hus-band. If you want to destroy a nation, get rid of the strong men, and then you can have your way with the rest of the people.

This has been the strategy Satan has used to catastrophic ends against black families. If we are going to fully engage in this battle for the souls of our young men, we must know the Enemy well. Consider his characteristics:

1. The Enemy is committed to his cause.

We may be confused and misdirected about our purpose, but Satan and his minions are organized and very strategic in their attacks. He is clear about his purpose and committed to it. He knows that the purpose of man is to glorify God, and he works night and day to make sure our families do not reflect God's glory.

2. The Enemy is patient.

Scripture describes Satan as a roaring lion, lurking about, seeking someone to devour. He waits until just the right point of vulnerability.

3. The Enemy will use our weaknesses against us.

Consider how Satan chose to attack Christ. He waited until Jesus had fasted for forty days and forty nights. He was physically weak. And it was at this strategic moment that he chose his attack. He does the same with us and our vulnerable young men.

4. The Enemy blends in.

It would be so much easier if he actually had a long tail and horns and carried a pitchfork. But, unfortunately, he is not that easily detected. He blends in by fanning the flames of our natural passions and desires. He plants thoughts in our minds that—if we are not careful—will lead to our own destruction.

5. The Enemy capitalizes on our lethargic "all is well" attitude.

Many of us sat back and watched as our impact on the family was marginalized by social programs, welfare, and systemic evils. We have not fought for our right to lead and provide. And while we have laid down our battle gear, Satan has wreaked havoc with our families and with our sons.

How Will You Respond?

It is this author's opinion that we should respond to the crisis facing our young men with the same energy and determination as was used to respond to the 9/11 crisis. No, we don't see buildings burning, but voices of young boys cry for their fathers. No, there is no presidential proclamation, but we have a mandate from history and motivation from the present. The time is now, and the task is ours if we will accept it.

A soldier is only responsible for those within his reach. He is not required to be successful on every battlefront but only the one where he is deployed. You and I have been deployed in our homes and communities for one reason, and that is to do battle.

In 1998 I obtained a copy of the suspension statistics for my local school district. The data indicated that for every white boy that was suspended from school, seven black boys were suspended, and we are only 30% of the population. In my mind, this was the equivalent of the KGB kicking in the door of my home and stating that they were taking all of the black boys away.

Armed with that information, I resigned my position as assistant pastor of Canaan Baptist Church and began an aggressive effort to help the boys in our local schools. Today we average one hundred mentors interacting with three hundred young people in our local school district. We have black children who are going to college because of the support and encouragement of their mentor. Other young people acknowledge that they would not have completed high school without the help of their mentor.

A soldier or warrior is one who seeks out the enemy. A soldier never waits for the enemy to come to him but goes on search-and-destroy missions. There is considerable controversy regarding the overseas wars that our nation gets involved in, but the point that most Americans agree on is that it is better for the soldiers to be over there fighting than for the enemy to be over here fighting. Let us take up the battle against our Enemy.

Soldiers Are Desperately Needed

What I envision is an army of men having a great impact their neighborhoods. This can be done when men take ownership of the problem. In other words, it is not the government's problem, nor some other guy's problem, but *our problem*! People often ask me why I am so motivated to help young men. I respond, "When I look at a young man, I do not see him. I see me. He is just as helpless and hopeless as I was at his age." This perspective makes me keenly aware of my own individual responsibility as a soldier in this crucial battle.

Work with the Mind-set of Individual Responsibility

This is key to solving the problem if we will accept it. What I mean by individual responsibility is trying to see every boy as our own. If this is not natural for you, you can train yourself to think this way. I suggest that you begin by asking God to give you His heart for young men. It is amazing how our attitudes about people change when we give God permission to love through us.

★ ★ ★

Whenever you encounter a young man, look him in the eye.

★ ★ ★

Whenever you encounter a young man, look him in the eye. This will help you connect with his soul. I promise that when you begin to see the emptiness in the souls of so many young men, it will affect you.

Looking at them this way also has an impact on the young men. I often look complete strangers under the age of seventeen in the eye.

They most often respond favorably to this, because many of them are not accustomed to having their souls viewed by the discerning eye of a mature man.

When you meet a young man, say to yourself, "It's not him, but me." In time, this practice will draw you closer to young men. I can promise you a richer life when you connect with them. Your scope will be broadened; your perspective on today's youth will be challenged and stimulated. And as each of us accepts our individual responsibility, we will be prepared to coalesce our efforts with other men.

Work in Concert with Other Men

I meet with men on a regular basis who are fellow soldiers of mine. We have the same goal of helping young men. I answer to them, and they answer to me. I encourage them, and they encourage me. All soldiers are strengthened when they know that other soldiers have their back.

The first time I was addressed as a soldier was when I was in Baltimore visiting the Maryland Mentoring Partnership. Selwin Ray approached me, stuck out his hand, and said, "How you doing, soldier?" Because I do not have a military background, I had several reactions to being called *soldier*:

- I was taken by surprise, because few people understand that we are in a war and that the title of soldier is appropriate for men who are committed to making a difference.
- I was shocked by the graphic nature of the title, the imagery it conjures up, and what it says about me.

- My heart was warmed by the clarity that comes with that title. Soldiers do not make excuses. Soldiers are trained to get the job done in spite of obstacles. Soldiers have a heart for the mother country and embrace the cause of their generation.

Well, soldier, how are you doing? It is my prayer that you will become motivated to action, because it is our turn to make a difference. I believe we can turn the negative trend facing young men if we work together. Proverbs 17:17 says, "A friend loveth at all times, and a brother is born for adversity."

As I said before, previous generations responded to their challenges, and now it is our turn. Consider what the following Scripture says about soldiers: "Thou therefore endure hardness, as a good soldier of Jesus Christ. No man that warreth entangleth himself with the affairs of this life; that he may please him who hath chosen him to be a soldier" (2 Timothy 2:3–4).

We can no longer only raise our own sons, but we must also raise the sons of our community. As I was writing this book I wanted to name it *Your Son and a Couple More*. I was advised to name it *Can I Call You Soldier?* but the main idea is that every man needs to be responsible for his son and a couple more young men. There is a war going on, and we must be alert to the conditions of the battlefield.

Become Alert to the Conditions

If we become keenly aware of how the condition of the youth of the larger society affects our families, we will be more motivated to do something. This was made clear to me on several occasions with my own children.

On one occasion I spoke at a church on the West Side of Chicago. I took my thirteen-year-old son with me. When we arrived at the church, men met us in the parking lot and proceeded to watch my car while I was inside. Once inside, my son went to sit with a group of boys his age. Meanwhile, I chatted with the pastor, who informed me that his church was helping that group of boys. He said that they were all in gangs, most had been incarcerated, and a few had killed people. I looked at my son who was sitting among them and thought, *I hope he does not say the wrong thing.*

Please note: you could not physically tell the difference between my son and the other boys. We don't know who will cross paths with our wives, sons, or daughters. We must be prepared at all times . . . and so must those we love. Your investment in a young man today can reap benefits for your children and even great-grandchildren. The need is urgent.

The ball is in our court. It is our turn.

★ ★ ★

Can I call you soldier?

★ ★ ★

ROLL CALL

☐ YES ☐ NO

1. Do you consider yourself a soldier?
Do not allow past failures to stop your involvement now.

☐ YES ☐ NO

2. Do you feel you have issues that would prevent you from being a soldier? Do not allow personal issues to prevent you from serving our youth. It is through serving in areas where we were once weak that we become strong.

☐ YES ☐ NO

3. The author stated that bad fathers raise confused sons.
Tell the truth and shame the Devil; were you raised by a bad father?

☐ YES ☐ NO

4. Everybody has father issues. Wise people deal with theirs so they can heal and not pass on the dysfunction to the next generation. Are you dealing with your father issues?

☐ YES ☐ NO

5. In your opinion, are the gatekeepers paying enough attention to fatherhood issues?

☐ YES ☐ NO

6. The author lists five characteristics of the Enemy. Based on those characteristics, would you say that the Enemy is a strong opponent? NFL teams meticulously study the plays and plans of the opposing team. Become a serious student of how the Enemy attacks you. Once you know his method of attacking you, you can better defend yourself and be better equipped to help others.

☐ YES ☐ NO

7. The author states that a copy of the suspension statistics from the local school system fired him up and got him totally involved with our youth. Have you experienced anything that has gotten you fired up to help our youth? What was it?

☐ YES ☐ NO

8. Do you take responsibility for where you are in life? Maintain a holy agitation regarding self-improvement. A soldier knows that on the battlefield his comrades are there to help him, but in the final analysis he has to fight for himself.

☐ YES ☐ NO

9. Has anyone ever called you a soldier or warrior because of your investment in the lives of others? If the answer is no, what do you plan to do about it?

★ ★ ★

With all of the uncertain voices screaming for the attention of boys today, the secure voice of a father [an involved soldier] is needed as never before.

Dr. Harold D. Davis

★ ★ ★

CHAPTER TWO

TELLING IT LIKE IT IS

While attending a pastors' conference, I encountered two young preachers from the Virgin Islands. They were curious about the title of my book *Talks My Father Never Had with Me*, and they wondered why I would write a book like that. They had difficulty understanding the idea that a man would not raise his own son, requiring others to get involved. I can still see the puzzled look on their faces as I awkwardly explained this nation's absentee father crisis.

As I talked with them, I thought how refreshing their perspective was. I began to ask myself, *Have we accepted and become comfortable with the current fatherhood crisis in America?* Since I wrote that book, my base of knowledge on father issues has expanded greatly. I am more convinced than ever that fatherhood in our nation is in a downward trend. America is leading the way when it comes to divorced fathers, absent fathers, and fathers who don't seem to care.

James 1:27 states: "Pure religion and undefiled before God and the Father is this, To visit the fatherless and widows in their affliction, and to keep himself unspotted from the world." I draw two points from this Scripture to show that fathers are critically needed:

1. Ministering to the fatherless is first on the list of activities of pure faith. The Bible clearly teaches that God has a heart for those who do not have fathers.
2. The fatherless and widows should be visited "in their affliction." In ancient times it was a great disadvantage not to have a father. Families who did not have fathers were often at risk from predators, poverty, and even starvation.

Today we have social programs to keep people from starvation and other abuses, but the social, emotional, and spiritual deficits of the fatherless are the same today as they were two thousand years ago. As we strive to be more like Christ, let us also seek His heart on fatherhood issues.

Something Important Is Missing

I never will forget the day I walked into the principal's office at Franklin Magnet Middle School. The principal was an attractive woman of stature. We had a good working relationship, and she could talk to me. This day, our encounter was different. I knocked on her office door, and she stuck her head out the door. Her eyes were red, her hair was frazzled, and she looked disgusted. I could see through the door that she had three young brothers in her office.

When she saw me, she fixed her eyes on me and said, "Reverend Davis, I have heard the African proverb that it takes a whole village to raise a child. I have the children. *Where is the village?!*" Then she closed the door. I stood there for a moment, thinking about what she said.

After some thought, I concluded that it is unfair for a woman serving at a school to have to deal with young men who are coming into adulthood without the aid of the community (men and fathers). Most problems found in our schools result from the fact that our boys do not have authority figures (functioning fathers) in their lives. This encounter was the catalyst that led me to start a mentoring program in her school. These kinds of programs are spreading across the nation.

Getting Involved

We have to move toward the tribal or communal fatherhood model, where all the men take responsibility for all the children in the village. When men begin to take the crisis personally and get involved, they become a source of help to the younger men around them with voids that need to be filled. The thesis statement of our mentoring program makes this point:

> Every boy needs a man in his face,
> challenging him with wisdom regarding
> critical issues and decisions in his life.

> EXPLANATION: Every boy needs a man who will firmly, unflinchingly, and lovingly correct him when he has made a bad decision. Our prisons are full of young men who had no one to get in their face, tell them that they were wrong, and then provide them with a solution.

We teach boys to memorize this quote in the third grade. The goal is for boys to learn that a man challenging them with wisdom is good, and it demonstrates love and concern.

When a man of influence and correction is not in a boy's life, the void will allow the boy to make more foolish decisions than he would otherwise have made. It is imperative that we face the battle, not turn from it. When it comes to the battle for our boys, don't be listed as AWOL or missing in action, but present and accounted for.

Men Teach Boys Principles

A man in a boy's life provides principles for the boy to live by. Rules are only animated, empowered, or respected because of a personality. In other words, the only reason many young men do the right thing (when they would rather do the wrong thing) is because there is a power, authority, or force waiting to pounce on them if they do not respond properly. This may sound barbaric, but during critical periods in a young man's life, the only thing he will respond to is a stronger man.

It is also true that during the period when a boy is making the transition to manhood, he will often refuse to listen to his mother. Most of the crisis calls that our office receives come from mothers of fifteen-year-old boys whom they can no longer control. During this season of life, the only thing that these young men will respond to is superior physical force. The role of enforcer has traditionally been played by the father. Most boys know that their father has a line that they'd better not cross, or he may snap. This deterrent has served for generations to help keep young men in check.

I clearly remember one occasion when my father thought that I got smart with my mother. I did not sass her, but he thought I did. He told me: "Son, I do not have any money to buy you any teeth, so don't make me knock the ones you have out." I understood exactly what he was saying, and I did not push those buttons anymore. My dad's authority and firmness ministered to me, keeping me in line and out of jail. That void in the lives of many of today's young men is reaping catastrophic consequences for our society.

Whenever you encounter someone who disses fathers and fatherhood, remember that this person is scarred. We must resurrect and celebrate the idea of healthy fathering in our communities. We must speak positively about it and be ready to demonstrate what it looks like and teach it to others.

Fatherhood Equals Unparalled Joy

When I attended Charleston High School I was young, foolish, and only concerned about being cool. My father worked less than a block away from the school, and I would occasionally see him. To my shame, I was often embarrassed at him because he was a janitor and would have dust cloths hanging out of his pockets or a broom in hand. I had no idea of how proud he was of me and how much he sacrificed to make my life as pleasant as possible.

★ ★ ★

A human father is supposed to model himself after our heavenly Father.

★ ★ ★

On many occasions I would run over to his job and ask for $1.50 for lunch. He would reach into his pocket and take out his last dollar bill and give it to me. In retrospect, I never saw any disgust or frustration on his face, but only joy. As a father I now realize that it was a joy for him to give his son all he had.

Just recently my daughter and I were riding in the car, and she stated that she was hungry and wanted a burger. She said that she would settle for McDonald's, but she really wanted Wendy's. For some reason, at that moment, I had a flashback and remembered my dad giving me his last dollar for a burger. I took her to Wendy's and, without taxing my budget, gave her the funds she needed to get her burger. As she went to get her burger, I could hardly contain the explosive feelings of gratitude for the example of my father, and I thanked God for allowing me to provide for my children.

A father takes great joy in sacrificially giving to his family. "Fear not, little flock; for it is your Father's good pleasure to give you the kingdom" (Luke 12:32). Society, primarily television, often portrays fathers as narcissistic and self-serving. Fathers who know about the heavenly Father have a different paradigm and the best conceivable role model.

It is time for our nation to start respecting fathers again, which will happen when fathers begin to earn that respect through sacrificially leading our families. A human father is supposed to model himself after our heavenly Father, who is love and never wavers. As men begin to do this, fathering will again become a coveted role in society. When a man works hard at his number one task of fathering, the results will be respect from his wife and children, and envy from those who look on.

I am delighted that volumes of books are now being written on this issue. It is not the goal of this small book to deal extensively with fatherhood issues, but only to whet your appetite and encourage your involvement. Continue to be excited about learning how to father your children, because you can never learn enough about how to father like God our Father. The challenge is on. The time is now. Let's respond quickly before we lose more innocent young men.

★ ★ ★

Can I call you soldier?

★ ★ ★

ROLL CALL

☐ YES ☐ NO

1. Are you committed to being the best possible father that you can be? Seek to be taught by older fathers, because fathering skills are learned only from fathers.

2. If the principal of the local middle school told you that she could not handle the boys in her school, what would you do?
Become a catalyst for change.
Volunteer, organize men, and make a difference.

☐ YES ☐ NO

3. Are you prepared to fight like a soldier to keep your family intact against internal and external forces? Raising a family is the most challenging task a man faces in life. Just as you strive for perfection on the job, *ballin'*, and in other pursuits, also make staying with the wife of your youth a priority.

☐ YES ☐ NO

4. Divorce has had a catastrophic impact on our nation. If you are a product of divorced parents, have you decided to aggressively deal with scars related to your parents' divorce? Determine that for you and your house, divorce is not an option.

☐ YES ☐ NO

5. Good fathering is not inherited; it must be learned. Have you had a good example of fathering? If no, what do you plan to do about it? Find a support group. It is a lie that you are all alone in your attempts to do it right. There are organizations out there that exist to help fathers fulfill their roles. There are books, tapes, Web sites, CDs, and other materials available to assist you. Take the initiative and seek them out.

☐ YES ☐ NO

6. The author spoke of the impact his father's giving has had on him. Are you planting seeds by sacrificially giving to your family? Fathering is a synonym for sacrifice. The key is to plug into God's resources, and you will never be without something to give to your family.

☐ YES ☐ NO

7. Do you agree with the author that the fatherhood crisis calls for drastic action? Put yourself in the shoes of the helpless boys. This will serve to motivate you to action.

☐ YES ☐ NO

8. As a result of reading this chapter, do you plan to do anything differently? Identify one area in your life where you need to improve, and ask God to help you improve in that area. It is also good to get an accountability partner to provide some assistance.

★ ★ ★

It takes years to
learn how to become a soldier
[a man who serves others]. Work
on it one day at a time.

DR. HAROLD D. DAVIS

★ ★ ★

CHAPTER THREE

A MAN WITHOUT FORCE

When I interact with young men in the public schools, I often use quotes as a focal point for discussion. When I interact with young men in the church, we dialogue around Scripture. One quote that challenges all of us comes from Frederick Douglass.

If you know your history, you are aware that Frederick Douglass endured some very challenging situations. In spite of being born in slavery, being denied the opportunity to learn to read, and all of the oppressions of that era, he persevered to become one of the greatest leaders of all time. When we consider his struggles and accomplishments, it makes most of us pretty quiet regarding what we have gone through. His struggles make his words all the more powerful as I read them. This is what he said about what constitutes real manhood:

> A man without force is without the essential dignity of humanity. Human nature is so constructed that it cannot honor a helpless man, although it can pity him, but even this it cannot do for long if signs of power do not arise.
>
> —Frederick Douglass, 1897

What Is Force?

When I first read this quote, it messed me up. I had to dissect it, meditate on it, and evaluate my life through the lens of this quote. I concluded that we have a crisis in our country and community because of the large number of men (old and young) who do not have force.

Please note how important Douglass says that force is. He calls it "the essential dignity of humanity." In other words, a man who does not have force does not possess basic human dignity. What is the opposite of "helpless"? It is *capable*. What is the opposite of weakness that is to be pitied? Douglass says it is "signs of *power*."

Well, the next questions I had to ask myself were: "What is force? What does it mean to be a man of force? How does that play out in life?" In my opinion, *force is an inner drive that is rooted in a basic understanding of life*. Force will motivate you because you fully understand the consequences of inaction.

Frederick Douglass says that when men do not have force, society will eventually marginalize them. To be marginalized is to be set aside, kicked to the curb, and overlooked. It is much like what adults do to children when they do not have time to deal with them right away. They put them off. Douglass ends his quote by stating that unless signs of power arise, man is not much use to society.

Every culture has valued its soldiers. There is a basic understanding that if there are no soldiers, our homes, families, and belongings can be taken from us, and we can be killed or made to be slaves. Douglass is saying that every man should have some soldier in him and serve his present generation. When I think of last names like Douglass, Carver, Marshall, King, Abernathy, Mandela, Powell, and many others, I am motivated to follow in their footsteps and place the benefit of the masses above my personal benefit. Soldiers do what they do for the benefit of the homeland and the home folks.

When young David first encountered the threat to Israel named Goliath, he asked the question, "Who is this uncircumcised Philistine, that he should defy the armies of the living God?" (1 Samuel 17:26). The reason he could do this was because he had unwavering confidence in God's commitment to his family and nation. I believe that many of our great ancestors worked for freedom with the same mind-set. The all-important question is, *What is our mind-set regarding the challenge to young black men in America?*

The Douglass quote stirs me because I have encountered so many men who had no force. If that weren't bad enough, I see a society that is forbidding young men to have drive to influence anyone or anything for good. This is tragic, because many young men today are heading for self-centered, impactless lives if nothing changes.

In my opinion, the subject of force in the lives of men should be shared every time we get a chance. Whenever I speak before an audience, I always touch on this subject. I feel so strongly about it that no matter whom I am speaking to, the subject of men and force comes up.

What amazes me is that this is a touchy subject and somewhat controversial. When you speak of men having force, some people get nervous. I realize that it is because of the abuse of force that people feel this way. It is tragic that weak men have abused their physical force against innocent women and children, most often their own families. We should never allow the abuse of a thing to condemn the proper use of it. When the subject of force is brought up in a healthy conversation, it is in the context of using force to benefit society and *never* to abuse people.

What Encourages Force

1. Hunger stimulates force.

A man who is initially provided for and fed by his mother and then by his woman has no need to cultivate force. Inner drive and motivation are necessary to legally secure the necessities of life. When everything is handed to a boy, he may grow to adulthood and never understand the need to work. Hunger is a great motivator for young men to become men of action. It is hoped that the motivation they get from hunger will move toward the dignity of work and not stealing.

2. Hope stimulates force.

Hope gives a man forward focus and drive. It is difficult to have force where there is no hope. Hope is born through faith in the possibilities of life. Many young men build their hope on the power of their own potential and the examples others have set for them. A boy who observes success in others hopefully will see their successes as proof that he can succeed.

★ ★ ★

Never lose hope in your dreams. For without dreams, life is a broken-winged bird that cannot fly.—Langston Hughes

★ ★ ★

Some young men are wise enough to view their existence as proof that anything is possible. With this belief, they see life as an endless series of opportunities designed to help them succeed.

3. Honor stimulates force.

Honor in families helps develop a healthy pride, which motivates a young man to move forcefully in the direction of his goals.

When a man is honored (not patronized) by society, his force will increase. Being validated by others is a very encouraging experience that generally increases a man's faith in his ability to achieve.

It is for this reason that mature men should encourage and compliment young men every chance they get. Honor is most powerful when it comes from one more powerful than the one being honored.

4. Heritage stimulates force.

Family relations, especially the relationship with his father, add value to a young man's existence. When a man can look behind him and around him to see loved ones (especially men) who held high standards, he can be motivated to follow in their footsteps.

What a Man Accomplishes with Force

He can stay with his wife. Only strong men can love women the way they need to be loved. In marriage, a man who is gentle, loving, and kind must be a man of force, because it takes understanding and strength to sacrificially love a woman. Force is needed to crucify self and put the family first. Don't let anybody fool you; to live sacrificially as Christ did requires the power that Jesus makes available to every man through His Holy Spirit.

He can control his passions. The need to control your passions is with you all your days. A young man needs to master the art of controlling his passions while he is young and continue to refine the art as he matures. The technology of the battlefield changes, but the war is the same. Soldiers who are not current with the latest modes of warfare perish on the battlefield. Issues with anger, sex, and ego attack us. It takes force and the power of God to harness them. The man of force must first recognize the attack, then respond with the appropriate weapons to defend his territory.

He can keep a job. When a man of force senses the urge to provide for his family, he uses it to seize opportunities for employment. He is not concerned if the job is not ideal, but he works that job until a better one comes along. His ability to keep a job is motivated by internal dignity and the external needs of his family. We have a crisis situation where many young men have not witnessed men persevering on the job. They need role models in this area.

★ ★ ★

People who do not understand that life is an uphill battle often see themselves as victims.

★ ★ ★

He is trustworthy. A man of force has no need to lie, because he can face the truth. He has no need to steal, because he is willing to work. He has settled the internal issues that would lead him to be untrustworthy:

- He understands that in the end he will face a Judge that is honest and fair and knows everything about everybody.
- He understands that integrity is strength. A young man of integrity told me that he was amazed that he received as much respect in the barbershop as men in their forties and fifties. Most young men have no appreciation for the invisible strength and power that is available to men of integrity. The man who understands the power of integrity has a tremendous advantage in life.

He has inner fortitude. He can overcome any obstacle that comes his way. People often ask me, "How is life treating you?" I tell them that life is designed to kick you in the butt. The question becomes, "How are you handling it?" People who do not understand that life is an uphill battle often see themselves as victims. Job made it plain to us when he said, "Man that is born of a woman is of few days and full of trouble" (Job 14:1). Because they do not understand the nature of our fallen world, many men become bitter, blame the system, or quit trying to get ahead.

His strength overflows into the lives of others. A man of force is seen as an oasis in the desert. Because he understands that all people are created in the image of God, he provides comfort to the weak and encouragement to the downtrodden. He can lift the mood of people when he walks into a room. Women see him as a source of hope, and strong men see him as an ally serving society from the masculine perspective. His life is like a cup that overflows: everything in the cup is for him and his family, and the overflow is for those around him who benefit from his rich life.

For the remainder of this book I will discuss subjects that are related to men having force. If you are challenged, that is a good thing. It is a good thing to keep company with strong men of force, because according to Proverbs 27:17, "As iron sharpens iron, so one man sharpens another" (NIV). As you read on, remember that our purpose is not to condemn men but to encourage and challenge them to be healthy men of force.

★ ★ ★

Can I call you soldier?

★ ★ ★

ROLL CALL

☐ YES ☐ NO

1. From your perspective, do you feel that you are a man of force?

☐ YES ☐ NO

2. Force is what Douglass called the "essential dignity" of manhood. Do you agree with him on this point?

☐ YES ☐ NO

3. Have you given any thought to how your relationship with your father has impacted the force that you have today?

4. Force can be acquired if you have none, and force can be increased if you have a little bit. What specific thing do you plan to do today to increase your force? Seek to develop your force by learning the biblical principles of manhood.

5. In your opinion, how is society teaching boys not to have force?

6. Why did the author say that society often fears men of force? Seek to become a gentle giant, and people will simultaneously respect your force, and feel comfortable and safe being around you.

7. In what areas of life has your forcefulness been most evident in society? (For example, as a father, as a wage earner, in sports, in personal integrity, etc.)

8. The author lists several qualities that give a man force. Name the quality that gives you force. Always help young men tap into their force and identify why they do or do not have any.

9. The author lists a few qualities of a man of force. How many of these qualities are present in your life? Make it a daily task to become more like your Savior every day.

★ ★ ★

Principles or rules that we disagree with are only obeyed when there is a powerful personality associated with the principle. In other words, if no man is around to enforce the rules of appropriate behavior, the fifteen-year-old boy will see no logical reason to obey them. Take time to become the powerful personality, the soldier, in the life of a young man.

DR. HAROLD D. DAVIS

★ ★ ★

CHAPTER FOUR

DEAL WITH THE FOOL IN YOU FIRST

Every man has a first order of business that he needs to take care of. This order of business should be priority number one from early childhood until the job is done. Some people would call this maturing; others would call it growing up. I like to call it *dealing with the fool that is in you.*

In my experience, men said hello to the fool in junior high school. Ideally, they say good-bye to him at high school graduation or in the early college years. Unfortunately, it is taking men longer to grow up, longer to address the dysfunctional trends in their lives, and thus the fool in them extends his reign well into adulthood. I believe that every man has a fool in him that must be tamed before he can be successful.

Let me take a moment to make my point. Have you ever done something foolish that was against your values and common sense? I have. I am talking about something really stupid. I later asked myself, "Why did I do that?" I have come to believe that it was the fool in me. "Foolishness is bound in the heart of a child; but the rod of correction shall drive it far from him" (Proverbs 22:15).

The Fool Is Destructive

This fool encourages me to do the self-destructive things that have become so common among black men. It has become almost commonplace for black boys not to have a father in the home and for expectant mothers to have to go it alone. This was pointed out very clearly to me when my wife became pregnant with our first child. She was still a college student and went to the hospital on campus. The doctor told her that she was pregnant and turned around and began to write. She asked him what was he doing, and he told her that he was preparing the paperwork for her abortion, at which point she replied: "I have a husband!" The doctor's mind-set and stereotypical response to a pregnant black woman has become all too common in our society.

The fool in black men is ultimately responsible for this condition. The voice of reason is always there to challenge the fool, but the voice of reason is always soft and polite, while the fool's voice is always booming. I am sure that you can identify men who were successful, but in a weak moment listened to the suggestion of the fool in them and found themselves in big trouble. I am convinced that until men learn how to neutralize the influence of that fool, we will not experience long-term success.

★ ★ ★

The fool is the old man, the flesh.

★ ★ ★

Many men find themselves helpless to give to the next generation because they are still dealing with the fool in them. For whatever reason, they did not have the support, knowledge, example, and guidance to neutralize the fool earlier in life. Now that they are in their thirties and forties, they find themselves doing what they should have done when they were younger. "When I was a child, I talked like a child, I thought like a child, I reasoned like a child. When I became a man, I put childish ways behind me" (1 Corinthians 13:11 NIV).

How to Address the Fool in You

REMEMBER, THE FOOL IS *NOT* YOU

The fool is the resident fallen nature that constantly seeks to control us. Paul struggled with this and came to understand it in Romans 7:17–18: "Now then it is no more I that do it, but sin that dwelleth in me. For I know that in me (that is, in my flesh,) dwelleth no good thing." I learned to consider the fool as a separate entity and not part of me. The fool is the old man, the flesh.

Paul also gives us the solution: "Our old man is crucified with [Christ], that the body of sin might be destroyed, that henceforth we should not serve sin. . . . For if ye live after the flesh, ye shall die: but if ye through the Spirit do mortify the deeds of the body, ye shall live" (Romans 6:6; 8:13). We are new creations by the power of Christ. So when I hear the suggestions and thoughts that originate with the fool, I immediately tell myself, "That is not me talking." Once I tell myself that, I no longer feel obligated to respond or be obedient to the fool.

On one occasion, I was standing at a teller window in the bank. The teller was counting a big wad of money. The fool screamed in my ear, "Grab it! Grab it! Grab it!" Please note that I have never had a problem with stealing, but that does not matter to the fool. He will try anything. I thought to myself, *Fool! I am not listening to you!* I began to realize that the fool in me is crazy, and he is easily identified because of the crazy things he tries to get me to do. Remember, the fool in you is not you.

Separate from the fool

If two individuals are destructive when they are together, separation is a good thing. How many times did your parents caution you regarding someone you were hanging out with? It is time that you discipline and remind yourself that you and the fool should not hang out together. What I mean by this is that you do not converse with him, and whenever you detect his presence, you immediately distance yourself from him. Of course, all of this takes place in the mind, and no one else is aware of it. Thoughts are powerful, and it is work to suppress foolish thoughts and not act on them.

Once you separate yourself from the fool, you begin to see him as an enemy who needs to be ignored. Please note: he may never completely go away, but he can be neutralized. The fool has always been there, and he is a good student of human nature, yours in particular. He knows where all of your hot buttons are, and he never tires of pushing them.

When you are challenged by the fool, I suggest that you behave like a little child I saw the other day. A one-year-old was being asked by a parent to do something that he did not want to do. In response the child turned his head and closed his eyes. In his mind, when he closed his eyes, the adult disappeared. I thought to myself, *That is a good tactic to use when the fool speaks.* We should close our ears to his voice and mentally move him far from us. Try it sometime.

Learn how to dis the fool

I have learned not to negotiate with the fool in me. Negotiating is futile, because he does not understand the art of compromise but wants full control. If he is given 5 percent control of your mind, he will continue to fight until he has all of you. With this in mind, there is only one thing to do with the fool, and that is to maintain a seek-and-destroy attitude. I believe this is why the apostle Paul said we need to be "casting down imaginations, and every high thing that exalteth itself against the knowledge of God, and bringing into captivity every thought to the obedience of Christ" (2 Corinthians 10:5).

Tactics to Keep You from Giving In

1. Learn to identify who is giving you advice.

I admit that I have studied the fool in me for years. At this point in my life, he has no surprises for me. I know how he is going to hit me when I am tired, when I am in the presence of women, when I have a pocketful of money, or when I am broke.

From the beginning of our earthly existence, we spend our time learning to recognize voices. The first voice we learn is the voice of our mothers. We then come to recognize the voice of family members and friends. Once we mature and get married, we generally are moved by the voice of the one that we love. I submit that there are additional voices that we need to recognize immediately. The first voice is the voice of God. Genesis 3:8 says, "And they [Adam and Eve] heard the voice of the Lord God walking in the garden in the cool of the day." Jesus, the Great Shepherd, describes His voice in John 10:3–5: "The sheep hear his voice; and he calls his own sheep by name and leads them out. And when he brings out his own sheep, he goes before them; and the sheep follow him, for they know his voice. Yet they will by no means follow a stranger, but will flee from him, for they do not know the voice of strangers" (NKJV). As my grandmamma would say: "His voice is so sweet."

There is another voice that we need to learn to recognize. His voice and the fool's voice give you the same kind of advice. They seem to work together in concert. Eve heard his voice when he said through the serpent: "Yea, hath God said, Ye shall not eat of every tree of the garden?" (Genesis 3:1). Eve's downfall was that she did not know that this was the voice of the adversary, the Devil. In my experience, his voice is often recognizable because he is usually loud, disruptive, and inconsiderate. His voice frequently makes me feel as if I am being hustled or pimped. Initially his voice sounds reasonable and exciting, but once you shine the light of truth on him, you begin to recognize his voice as the voice of deception and destruction, as Eve well learned.

I heard an old preacher say that he is the same old Devil in a different dress. In other words, all his tactics are deceptive at the core but may vary in outward appearance. Remembering that he is the same old Devil will help you tire of his diabolical delicacies sooner.

The Evil One will do whatever he can to go against the things that are beneficial in the long run. He will try to get you to take shortcuts and reach goals before God's time. Just like the fool, he tries to get us to focus on our own needs and not the needs of others.

The Devil and the fool play on our emotions, trying to get us to make emotional decisions rather than calmly thinking things through. Haste is their mode of operation. Just like the salesman who wants you to make a decision while he has you on the phone—before you can settle down and think about it—the fool wants you to jump at the Enemy's suggestions in the heat of the moment.

Put ideas under the scrutiny of time. In other words, ask yourself, "If I do this, what is going to happen later?" Any truth claim can be verified when you consider the outcome of that truth over time. If you work at it, you can identify evil tactics and avoid them. Like in any battle, the warrior has to have various scenarios in mind depending on what the enemy does.

2. Rehearse what happened last time you listened to the fool.
All of us can remember times when we listened to the fool. The fool had convinced me that his way was the best way, and I followed his lead in various areas of my life. That was a very dangerous and destructive period for me. The fool does not want you to consider history when you are listening to him.

3. Study the lives of men who are slaves to the fool.
It is unfortunate that some men joined forces with the fool that is in them at an early age. They have known no other lifestyle. Others have given up fighting the fool and are total slaves to him. These men need help and hope to enable them to move beyond the reach of the fool that is in them.

I have had many conversations with men who have spent time in prison, done drugs, done the gang scene, and engaged in other pathological behaviors. Now that they have their lives together, they refer to that period in their lives as "being in their madness." I like to call it "pimped by the fool in me."

Immature men are regular victims of the fool in them. Wise, mature men master the fool in them and then turn to help other young men who have not figured it out yet.

Learn to question your actions and always filter the thoughts through the grid of biblical truth. When orders come to your mind requesting you to say or do something, ask yourself the question, "Who is speaking?" Consider it for a while to see if the command fits with Paul's list of the fool's ways: "Now the works of the flesh are evident, which are: adultery, fornication, uncleanness, lewdness, idolatry, sorcery, hatred, contentions, jealousies, outbursts of wrath, selfish ambitions, dissensions, heresies, envy, murders, drunkenness, revelries, and the like" (Galatians 5:19–21 NKJV). If it fits these criteria, don't do it; consider it a command from the fool that is in you.

4. STICK AND MOVE.

In all forms of warfare there is the concept of attacking the enemy, then moving from the spot of attack to avoid retaliation. In boxing this is called "stick and move." I believe that Christian warriors must learn the spiritual form of stick and move. Romans 12:1–3 is my life Scripture. It is the passage that God first made real to me that turned my life upside down. Verse 2 says: "And be not conformed to this world: but be ye transformed by the renewing of your mind, that ye may prove what is that good, and acceptable, and perfect, will of God."

When we sense the fool's attack, we need to immediately renew our mind with the Word of God and then move from the spot of attack. This may mean turning the TV off, disengaging from a conversation, leaving a party early, or fleeing any situation that empowers the fool and puts you at risk.

In order to stick the fool with the Word of God you will need to hide the Word in your heart. It is for this reason that Bible study is very important. There are men's Bible studies popping up in churches and organizations all over the country. I want to suggest that if your wife knows more about the Word than you do, lay your pride aside and ask her to help you get up to speed. When I met my wife, I was newly saved and she was already well versed in the Word. It required very aggressive Bible study on my part to become conversant with her.

In reality, the fool is no problem if he is handled properly, but the only proper way to handle the fool is with all that God makes available to you and with all of your might. If you do this, the fool will lose influence with every passing day as you "grow in grace, and in the knowledge of our Lord and Saviour Jesus Christ. To him be glory both now and for ever. Amen" (2 Peter 3:18).

★ ★ ★

Can I call you soldier?

★ ★ ★

ROLL CALL

☐ YES ☐ NO

1. Tell the truth and shame the Devil: Does the fool in you still run a significant portion of your life? Do a thorough self-evaluation to determine the influence the fool has in your life. This may require asking loved ones and friends for an honest evaluation of you. It may be uncomfortable and will require that you be vulnerable. Feel the pain, and go on.

☐ YES ☐ NO

2. First Corinthians 13:11 speaks of being a child and doing childish things. It also speaks of growing up and putting childish things away. Have you put away childish things? Spend some time with a few junior high school boys. This may assist you in seeing clearly the fool's method of manipulating and enslaving young men. Consider mentoring or volunteering with young men in some capacity.

3. Proverbs 22:15 speaks of foolishness in the heart of a child and the role the rod plays in driving it out of him. In your opinion, how has the prohibition against the rod (corporal punishment of spankings in school and/or the home) affected many of the young adults today?

☐ YES ☐ NO

4. Can you quickly identify the lie when a TV show mocks masculinity by making men look foolish? Become a vocal critic of TV shows that portray men as fools. A brief look at a few television shows will reveal men who are dominated by the fool in them. Normally, the man will do something foolish and the laugh track will play as if it were very funny. Young men cannot see through this attack, and many young men model their lives after these sitcoms.

☐ YES ☐ NO

5. Can you identify the voice of the fool in you? To help you do this, surround yourself with wisdom. Read at least one proverb from the book of Proverbs in the Bible every day. It is also good to read the autobiographies of great men.

☐ YES ☐ NO

6. Have you studied and become familiar with how the Enemy attacks you? The attacks have kept current with modern technology, but the vices haven't changed. Study the strategies that the Enemy has used on biblical characters and the men that are in your life. He will use the same strategies on you as he used on Job, David, and others.

7. What happened the last time you did what the fool told you to do? Think about our prison system, even the local jail, and understand the consequences of listening to the Devil.

☐ YES ☐ NO

8. The author states that most men say hello to the fool in junior high school. Do you remember when you said good-bye to the fool? Always be still and listen when older, wise men talk. They are a wonderful source of wisdom.

★ ★ ★

Let the record show that
children play. Mature men
[those who have accepted their role as a soldier]
stand in the face of all odds
and stay with their families.

DR. HAROLD D. DAVIS

★ ★ ★

CHAPTER FIVE

PLAYERS AND FAMILY SLAYERS

I remember the look in her dad's eyes when I came home with his daughter—a look of anger mixed with resignation. She was sweet sixteen and my first real girlfriend. Twenty-five years and three daughters later, I now understand what he went through while I dated his daughter. Although I was a good kid, no kid is really good enough to date your daughter.

Now, I am the man with not one daughter, but three daughters! I cringe at the statement that a man reaps what he sows. I have lived long enough to witness that it is true. No man establishes a lifestyle void of consequences—they are waiting for every man down the road. I now understand why my father would occasionally put his head down and say, "Have mercy, Father; have mercy."

One definition of the word *play* is "to act in a specified way; especially to pretend to be." While I realize that the street pronunciation of the related word *player* is "playa," and there are other, cruder definitions, since I view what it represents as playing, we will use the term *player* for this chapter.

A player is a person who is pretending to be something he is not, usually living a lifestyle that has no future to it. The concept of players or playing goes against everything that a father stands for. Young men today brag about *playin'* as if it were something to be proud of.

Unfortunately, it is only when a man matures that he can see the foolishness of it all. I was young and foolish at one time, and I listened to all the lies that young men are told about how to treat women. It is unfortunate that most young men fail to see the emptiness of the player's lifestyle until they are much older and have done considerable damage to many beautiful young women. Consider the truth in the following statement:

> Young men are not naturally programmed to know what to do with a young woman. If they follow their fleshly, egotistical, sexual instincts, the woman will be abused overtly or covertly, physically or psychologically. Mature men must teach young men the fine art of loving a woman.

Today's player mentality has the current generation of young men without hope and in bondage, just as the slaves in Egypt or America were without hope and in bondage. The following statement by Frederick Douglass speaks to those of us who can help the young men extricate themselves from their chains:

> If there is no struggle, there is no progress. Those who profess to favor freedom and yet deprecate agitation are men who want crops without plowing up the ground; they want rain without thunder and lightning. They want the ocean without the awful roar of its many waters. This struggle may be a moral one, or it may be a physical one, and it may be both moral and physical, but it must be a struggle.

> Power concedes nothing without a demand. It never did and it never will. Find out just what any people will quietly submit to and you have found out the exact measure of injustice and wrong that will continue till they are resisted with either words or blows or with both. The limits of tyrants are prescribed by the endurance of those whom they oppress. . . . Men may not get all they pay for in their world, but they must certainly pay for all they get.

Many points are made in this quote that I feel provide guidance for our response to the current dilemma. I want you to consider the following:

- "Power concedes nothing without a demand." The power of the player mind-set will not release the young men over to the church because we quote a few Bible verses and ask for them. We must demand them to come to Christ and go get them!
- Secondly, men today allow the tyranny of fatherlessness and oppression that plague our young men. Deliverance for our young men will come only when mature men pull the rope of this tyrant and loosen his grip on his prey.

Players are dangerous people who damage present and future marriages. I speak from the position of a marriage counselor who has confronted many couples who were trying to recover from an early experience with a player (male or female). The fact of the matter is that when a player has sex with a woman who is not his wife, he is stealing from her future husband. That wife will have to live with that unpleasant memory and the pain associated with being *played* for the rest of her life.

A healthy man understands his role as protector, provider, and pleaser and will want to secure a promising future for himself, his family, and his neighbor's family. He will want a woman who has not been damaged by men who only used her for fun and scarred her emotionally and physically. In my experience as a counselor I have come to agree with God that it is best if people delay sex until marriage. When this happens, there are no past memories for the present spouses to compete with.

I was born just after Woodstock and during the "free love" movement. This movement was wrong. My generation (who bought the free love lie) has come to understand that there was no free love, but that somebody (mostly women) paid for all the so-called love that was given.

If you are a player or desire to be a player, I want to encourage you to reconsider. The evidence points to the incredible pain and suffering that has resulted from that mind-set. We are in need of stayers, not players. America in general and the black community specifically is in critical need of men who love women and father the children they bear.

How to Resist the Player Urge

1. Find a support group.

We have all seen the movies where one man is so bad that he takes on an army by himself. We should remember that in real life those types of heroics are very rare. In reality, we are all very fragile—if not physically, then emotionally. The fact of the matter is *we all need help.*

I learned an important lesson from two men who had moral failures. They both cheated on their wives and greatly damaged the lives of many people. I noticed characteristics that were common in both of them: they were arrogant and self-sufficient, and neither of them listened to the counsel of friends *or* their woman.

After observing their lives implode, I concluded that I would be open and transparent to a few mature friends who loved me, and I would listen to the good advice my wife gives me. Women are very good at letting us know when we are getting a big head. I occasionally suffer with this problem and have learned to use my wife's perspective to stay balanced and keep a healthy male ego.

2. Don't let your failures stop you.

Failure has been called the back door to success. I must say that this is true for me. I have failed many times at different things. I can still see the looks of disappointment on the faces of people as they watched me when I failed. Many of us remember the pain of letting the team down or can think back to failures at school. My most painful failures (to date) have been not doing more of what my father asked me to do. I now realize that his words were rich with wisdom and pregnant with potential for success.

I have forgiven myself for that youthful indiscretion but live with the consequences of my actions. One key factor to consider when you fail is the breathing factor. If you are still breathing, it is not all that bad, because you can start again.

The ability to start over comes from deep within. No external motivation can keep you going against the odds, only a drive from the inside. This drive is related to the mental images you have planted in your mind. When you can see mental images of your goals, they can serve as motivation to keep you going. Strength can often be found in the examples of other men: men like your father, brother, mentor, or pastor who persevered when the odds were against them.

We follow the example of saints before us and, best of all, Christ's example. As we face our failures, we dust ourselves off and pursue God's goals for us. The apostle Paul's confession is for today's solider too:

> *Not that I have already attained [all God has for me], or am already perfected; but I press on, that I may lay hold of that for which Christ Jesus has also laid hold of me. Brethren, I do not count myself to have apprehended; but one thing I do, forgetting those things which are behind and reaching forward to those things which are ahead, I press toward the goal for the prize of the upward call of God in Christ Jesus.* —Philippians 3:12–15 NKJV

The bottom line is that our current situation requires that all men rise up from past failures and find strength for the challenge that is before them.

3. Learn to ignore the negative images.

There is a concerted move afoot to portray men in a negative light. Hollywood is very aggressive in its attempts to promote mindless players and effeminate men who have no interest in women. For the most part, TV is negative and mindless and does not serve to promote healthy masculinity. I am not saying that you should not watch TV, but I am saying that if you have not matured to the point where you can watch it with a discerning eye, you may want to curtail much of your TV time.

If you are having a problem with what I am saying, I want to challenge you to watch a few shows and commercials, keeping a paper and pencil handy. Take time to mark the number of times a man makes a mindless comment and the laugh track runs. Mark how many times a woman puts a man down because of something he says or does. Observe how many fathers are made to look clueless, and how many young men see family life as unfathomable or undesirable.

I believe that any man who exposes himself to this type of stimuli day in and day out will eventually be influenced by it. I am an ordained minister who for many years has read the Bible daily, but I must be careful what I expose myself to, because it will get into my subconscious. I often see those negative images in my mind on Sunday mornings when it is time to preach.

Subconscious messages have impacted a whole generation of young men. They have no idea what is involved in becoming a real man. Only the wise are able to extricate themselves from these negative influences.

4. Dream of heading a family that adores you.

It is a nontransferable, inexplicable joy to be a good husband and father. Personally, I would not trade this joy for any amount of money, prestige, or fame. There is an incredible respect that a woman has for a man who has been faithful to her for 5, 10, 15, 20, 25, or 30 years and beyond. Although she is his most stringent critic, she is also his most formidable supporter.

When children are small they look up at you with big eyes and say, "I luvs you, dadee." Once again, no joy can compete with this. Many men do well in the beginning of this race—producing children and being there for a while. But let me tell you the joy of going the distance. One of the greatest tests of fatherhood is the ability to finish well.

When grown children stand up and say, "My father is the greatest man on the face of the earth," and mean it, that man has done a great job. Grown children understand some of the struggles their parents went through to raise them. As adults, they will either work to understand why their father failed to stay and raise them, or they will delight as they begin to understand some of the incredible challenges he overcame to stay and raise them. Grown children give a true assessment of the job that a father does.

★ ★ ★

Men who build dynasties have the mind-set of "wife and children first."

★ ★ ★

Our society does not consider the benefits that accrue to a man who focuses on his family. There is no greater benefit to a mature man than a family that adores him. They will be proud to carry on his strong name.

5. FIND STRENGTH IN GOD.

Jesus Christ was the God-man among men. Although He did not have a family, we can learn family principles from how He loved His disciples (the equivalent of the modern-day church). Consider the fact that He put them before others.

Synonymous with being a father is to put his family before other people and things. I have been married for twenty-five years, and last year I had the privilege of buying a new car. This was the first time that I was able to get a new car, because for the last twenty-five years, emphasis was given to what was best for my wife and kids. I was blown away when I was finally able to purchase the car I wanted, even in the color I wanted! The whole family celebrated with me, and I realized that now that the kids are older, I could get some of the things

I always wanted. In this "me first" generation, we must help men understand that players have a "me first" attitude. But men who build dynasties have the mind-set of "wife and children first." Jesus Christ had a "family of God first" mind-set that we need to imitate.

Jesus also loved the church sacrificially. This type of love is an empowering love. It actually grants you the power to give more when you feel that you have given all. That *more* comes from a relationship with Christ. I learned this when I saw my father continue to serve his family during difficult times. His strength came from a relationship with God, which gave him the power to do what should be done. Strong men are able to put the needs of others (especially women and children) before their own needs. Just as Jesus derived great joy in meeting our needs, we should learn to derive great joy in meeting the needs of the young men.

In final analysis, playin' is for immature men who are not strong enough to be stayers. Staying with one woman and meeting her needs in a for-life commitment requires the supernatural strength that comes from God. Someone may say, "I know a man who stayed with his woman, and he did not have a relationship with God." My response is that he was a strong man who stayed with his woman. But the ultimate joy is for the man to stay with his woman on earth and then, in God's time, transition with her into heaven. This man must know Jesus and lead his family in the narrow path.

The challenge for our generation of men is to stay and not play.

★ ★ ★

Can I call you soldier?

★ ★ ★

ROLL CALL

☐ YES ☐ NO

1. Have you matured past all desires to be a player? Seek help from Jesus. Plainly tell Him your concerns, read the Bible, and watch God begin to do a work in your heart.

☐ YES ☐ NO

2. Are you the father of a daughter? If so, pray specifically for God to give you wisdom as you fulfill your role. As I am completing this book we are preparing for the wedding of my oldest daughter. Through God's graciousness, she is marrying a godly young man. Milestones such as these are paydays in the lives of good fathers.

☐ YES ☐ NO

3. Are you bold enough to challenge young men who want to be players? Every time you are around young men, seek an opportunity to challenge them to take the high road instead of the low road.

☐ YES ☐ NO

4. The author stated that he was born in the post-Woodstock "free love" era. Have you overcome the negative, sinful lifestyle of the era you were born in? Awareness is the first step to overcoming any negative lifestyle. It is through the Word of God that we become more aware of sinful thinking and habits that need to change.

☐ YES ☐ NO

5. Are you haunted by failures from your past? One of the Enemy's favorite tools is the monkey wrench from our past. He loves to bang us over the head with it, holding us in bondage to previous weaknesses. When you experience guilt from the past and can't shake it, go see your pastor or other mature brother in the Lord for help.

☐ YES ☐ NO

6. Do you have supportive friends who encourage you in your current (or future) role as a husband and father?
If the answer is no, are you willing to develop those types of friendships?

☐ YES ☐ NO

7. The author spoke of personality traits that were present in his two friends who had moral failures. Are you arrogant, self-sufficient, or unwilling to listen to the counsel of others?
If the answer is yes, what steps are you taking to change?

☐ YES ☐ NO

8. Do you have a family that adores you? Develop the mind-set that "family comes first." What are some actions you could take to demonstrate your family's prominent position?

★ ★ ★

A boy never forgets it when a man lovingly challenges him with an affectionate, intense finger in his face. This soldier may be his father, coach, teacher, uncle, or mentor; but the effect is the same.

DR. HAROLD D. DAVIS

★ ★ ★

ingrained in the minds of Christians that if you want to make most Christians tremble, just walk up to them and say "separation of church and state" and they will shudder.

The framers of the Constitution only wanted to protect the church from being controlled by the state and the state from being controlled by the church. As you view the nations that are governed by the Christian church or any religion, you see the faults of that system. The same is true when the church is ruled by the government. We don't want to mix the two, but they can complement each other. Most people who are involved with our schools agree that they could benefit from some *thou shalt nots.* Thou shalt not steal, kill, or covet would be a few to get started with.

A Pro-Gay Environment

I do not believe that most fathers realize that we now have a condition where, in many middle and high schools, a gay man can counsel their son in regards to sexual issues. In most cases it can be done without the fathers' permission or knowledge. Many fathers do not consider the fact that their sons might spend more time with a gay teacher in the public school than with their father.

I was taken by this fact when my middle-school daughter (who grew up in a Bible-reading and Bible-teaching home) came home and told me that gay people were born gay and they could not help it. This is a position supported by the gay community but not by medical science. She proceeded to tell me that her teacher (who was gay) told her that. Children will often believe an influential, popular teacher over their parents. There is an attempt to use the public schools to groom children to embrace the gay lifestyle. The question is, what are we doing to see to it that the children get all the information, not just the pro-gay perspective?

There is nothing new about the gay lifestyle. It was around when I grew up, and it was in my family. What's new and needs to be addressed is the aggressive nature in which radical gays are going after our children. I believe that soldiers need to stand in the gap between innocent boys and the gay men who would prey on them. Much of the grooming and contact starts in the primary grades of the public schools.

One thing that men understand is sex. We also understand how important the first sexual information and experience is. The details of sexual encounters are vividly remembered. If a boy learns about or experiences sex at the hands of a sick man, he is impacted for life and may struggle with his sexual identity for years to come. Soldiers must be vocal in their opposition to this.

Mentoring Opportunities in the Public School

For some, public schools are wonderful places of discovery. But for others, they seem to be jungles filled with dangers behind every tree. It has been my experience that a mentor can have an incredible impact on a young person with a limited amount of personal investment. Adults often forget the influence they can have. I just want to remind you that it doesn't take much to impress and affect a child for life.

Mentoring comes in many varieties. I have come to appreciate content-based mentoring, the type that we do with the *TALKS Mentoring Program.* Content-based mentoring is teaching. When mature adults are around children, teaching should be the primary activity.

Children are in desperate need of wisdom. All wisdom finds its origin in God and has come down through the generations as the most reliable way to live and survive in this sin-cursed world.

Knowledge is the accumulation of facts; wisdom is knowing when and where to use the knowledge. Children get wisdom either from hard knocks or from wise adults. Wisdom on issues related to masculinity best comes from men who have experience on their side. Transformation will happen when men begin to assume responsibility for younger men and take a few under their wing for safety and guidance. Only then will we see a new generation of wise men arise.

★ ★ ★

Experience is the best teacher, but it uses you up in the learning process.

★ ★ ★

The statistics indicate that the highest percentage of mentors belongs to the "twenty-one-year-old white female" demographic. The zeal of these women to be a part of the solution is commendable, but boys are in greater need of male mentors than female mentors. If men had some of the insight and zeal that women have to mentor, we could take care of the problem in record time. I appreciate all of the women who serve boys in the public schools of America, but it is time that men take up their rightful positions as the role models for young men.

Experience is the best teacher, but it uses you up in the learning process. It is best that we all learn from teaching and example rather than experience. Then, we can allow our experiences to confirm what we have been taught. This is why men should be excited about sharing wisdom with boys. I clearly and fondly remember Mr. Jenkins' finger in my face and in the face of all the boys in his shop class at Roosevelt Junior High School. We knew that he cared about us, and he would put an intense finger in our faces when we needed it. When boys embrace the wisdom of their mature male teachers, they are saved from many deadly pitfalls.

In the early 1980s, many school administrations had an air of superiority about them. They felt as if they had all they needed to educate children, and they would tell non-educators, "We don't need your help." Today that has changed, and schools desperately need male volunteers. Please begin to see yourself as a repository of wisdom that is available to the next generation. Accept the challenge to dispense your wisdom in a systematic way to young men. Opportunities abound for soldiers to make a difference.

★ ★ ★

Can I call you soldier?

★ ★ ★

ROLL CALL

☐ YES ☐ NO

1. Did you have a good elementary school experience?
Why or why not?

☐ YES ☐ NO

2. Are you already involved in the local schools? Consider visiting a school once a week to support a female teacher who has a lot of boys in her class. You do not have to say or do anything; just go and sit in the room and be pleasant.

☐ YES ☐ NO

3. Do you routinely celebrate young men who make good grades? Find some boys to encourage and reward for their academic excellence. It is a fact that black boys are frequently not celebrated by black men for their academic accomplishments.

☐ YES ☐ NO

4. Are you aware of the godless nature of most of our schools?

☐ YES ☐ NO

5. Are you willing to mentor or, better yet, start a mentoring program where you coordinate several mentors? Contact Dr. Davis to get information on how he built a program with over one hundred mentors.

☐ YES ☐ NO

6. Do you see yourself as a repository of wisdom?
Realize that you have a lot to offer men
who are as fewer than five years younger than you are.

☐ YES ☐ NO

7. We know that not all schools are godless, but the
overall mood and laws of the country tend to downplay
the benefits of godliness. Will you determine to be an
advocate for God whenever you get the chance?

☐ YES ☐ NO

8. Do you know how to challenge a truth claim?
Asking the following question can test all truth claims:
"If everybody did this, would we survive?"
Truth hurts when you are in opposition to it.
The success in positioning the gay lifestyle in an acceptable
light does not change the truth regarding the lifestyle.
Determine to become knowledgeable on how to articulate
a compassionate yet uncompromising position on gay issues.

To Contact Dr. Harold Davis:

KJAC Publishing
PO Box 111
Champaign, IL 61824
kjac-publishing.com
1-800-268-5861

★ ★ ★

Cowardice asks the question,
"Is it safe?"
Expediency asks the question,
"Is it politic?"
But conscience asks the question,
"Is it right?"
And there comes a time
when one must take a position
that is neither safe, nor politic,
nor popular but because
conscience tells one it is right.

DR. MARTIN LUTHER KING JR.

★ ★ ★

CHAPTER SEVEN

ENGAGING EVERY BLACK CHURCH

In the black community, the local church has always been a place where the problems of the community were taken and solutions were sought. In past years, this has been true of most communities in America. In view of the current dilemma with our young men, we need to look to the church for solutions and the resources to implement them.

In the past, the cry hurled from black pulpits was "We Shall Overcome!" I submit that the cry for our generation should be updated to "We Must Save Our Boys!" The following poem clearly makes this point:

Little Jimmy Lewis

I saw little Jimmy Lewis standin' on the corner today.
To stand on the corner is to broadcast to everyone
where your allegiance lay . . .
Jimmy grew up in this church; he was loved and well-known.
It seems that Jimmy has chosen a wandering path of his own.
Kids today seem to do that once they get halfway grown . . .

I saw little Jimmy Lewis standin' on the corner today . . .
You remember Jimmy; he used to sing the song
"The Lord Will Make a Way."
I believe he started having problems when he became an adolescent . . .
His dad was not home to challenge him;
the school said he was a manic depressant.
With pressure from the negative crowd and the enticements of the day,
Jimmy began to drift further from Jesus, the true and living way . . .
Jimmy passed through the wide gate where there is a party goin' on . . .
You can be sure that like the prodigal in the far country,
a day of reckoning will come.

I saw little Jimmy Lewis standin' on the corner today! . . .
He turned his head when he saw me comin'
and I continued on my way . . .
What can I do to help him, and do I have the nerve,
To lovingly challenge him to choose this day whom he will serve.

Should I tell the church, pastor, and the mothers?
It seems like they should know
That another child from our church has deviated
from the way that he should go.
What can the church do when we face such a trying hour?
The word on the street is that the church ain't got no power.

If we called Jimmy's momma, Sister Mable, and Aunt Ruth,
maybe the three of them could pray for Jimmy and
we could see what God would do.

Then we could call Brother Kendal; you know he has always been cool.
Maybe he could talk to Jimmy; maybe he could get through.

I saw little Jimmy Lewis standing' on the corner today . . .
Our Jimmies are in trouble, and that's a statistical fact.
But what the statistics don't show is how that
Jimmy's problem messes up Joslyn's act.
What's Joslyn supposed to do while Jimmy is
caught up in pathological behavior?
She can get mad or she can be bad; either way,
the odds are not in her favor.
Black women need black men to help them along the way.
Yes, Joslyn needs Jimmy just like we needed somebody back in the day.
There is a war goin' on to save our next generation.
Are you active in the battle for our youth, or are you just spectatin'?
Let us pray, brothers and sisters, for the Jimmies in our churches.
Let us organize into groups to search them out before Satan takes them.
I saw Little Jimmy Lewis standin' on the corner today . . .

As a member of a local congregation, you must become a soldier battling to make this story a rare occurrence rather than an everyday event. You need to fight for more activities for the kids. Encourage the leaders to spend more money on them. Admonish the men and church leaders who are narcissistic and self-serving to suffer (put up with) the little children as Jesus did in Matthew 19:14: "Jesus said, Suffer little children, and forbid them not, to come unto me: for of such is the kingdom of heaven." The church should model Christ's attitude and actions regarding children.

Steps for Your Church

1. Start a men's group.

A weekly or monthly men's fellowship will do much to strengthen the resolve of men who want to make a difference in the church and in the larger community. Encouragement is a major need of many men today. Not only will there be encouragement in a men's group, but there will also be empowerment. Men often are empowered by the positive men around them. "He that walketh with wise men shall be wise: but a companion of fools shall be destroyed" (Proverbs 13:20).

I enjoy being in the presence of strong men. I am always challenged to take my game to a higher level as a result of their presence. This type of positive stimulation is critically needed in our contemporary culture because of the large number of men who did not have a father around as they grew up. In a natural setting, the boy grows up impressed by his father's strength and later grows up to be his father's friend. Together they grow and continue to be impressed by the mystery and majesty of masculinity. The church that I attend has had a men's class for over twenty-five years, and it is a settled fact that the men who regularly attend this class have good marriages.

2. Start a substance-abuse ministry.

I believe that it is critical for more churches to design programs for those suffering from substance abuse. Several things happen when churches get involved in this area:

- *The credibility of the church within the community skyrockets.* Unfortunately, in recent years, many churches have lost their connection and influence with the nonchurched community.

A substance-abuse ministry will help rebuild credibility. When a family sees that their loved one is clean and sober (often for the first time in years), they know that it took a greater power than their own to make it happen. When the recovered drug addict begins to praise God and speak of the deliverance that has taken place in his life, God is seen not as a distant unconcerned deity, but as a God who is close, caring, and concerned. I know of several churches that are called to this ministry, and the impact on the church and community has been amazing.

- *Evangelism occurs when unchurched families become involved.* People are not interested in attending churches that just talk about doing something; they flock to churches that really are doing something.
- *The new members bring a fresh vibrancy to the whole body.* No church is designed to exist without an occasional infusion of new members. It is a fact that new members shake up old members and force the church to move forward.
- *When the soldiers in the church help their weaker brothers, respect for men in society, the church, and home increases.* Society is in need of men who are strong and caring. Once this man is identified, people will honor and follow him.

When the soldiers of previous generations faced the civil rights struggle, they focused on the sections of the Bible that addressed those issues. For example, Dr. King preached Amos 5:24, which says, "But let judgment run down as waters, and righteousness as a mighty stream." Before he quoted that verse, most Bible students had never even read the book of Amos.

I believe that we need to popularize Bible verses that speak to our contemporary problems, such as James 1:27 mentioned in chapter two and Malachi 4:6: "And he shall turn the heart of the fathers to the children, and the heart of the children to their fathers, lest I come and smite the earth with a curse." Of course there are many other Scriptures that you can quote and promote. Evangelistic Scriptures interjected in conversations about our youth are especially appropriate.

3. Make youth evangelization a lifestyle and a priority.

It has been my experience that young people are looking for caring adults to step into their lives. On one occasion, I was in the principal's office at a local high school. I noticed a young man who was a complete stranger. I walked up to him, and with concern in my voice, looked him in the eye and said, "You're not in trouble, are you?"

He responded, "No, I'm just getting a pass to go to class."

I put my hand on his shoulder and said, "Good, because I need for you to take care of business and represent up in here with some good grades." I then shadowboxed with him and walked away. As I left, I overheard him say, "I like men like that."

What he was actually saying was, "I appreciate the fact that he took some time with me, talked to me, and touched me." Statistics show that young black men are not touched by older men. This is tragic. Even my dog likes to be touched, and most owners will give their dogs some attention every now and then. Unfortunately, many young black men don't see caring faces, hear concerned voices, or experience positive physical contact from older black men. Showing concern doesn't cost anything, and we can meet that need. In order to be an effective soldier, you must care.

Evangelism will happen when people feel cared about. Jesus met the physical needs of people first, and then He talked about the soul. Boys need to feel that men care about them, and they need to feel challenged by men. These needs are not a line item in the budget—they are free.

4. Work to make marriages stronger.

We all know that marriage is under attack. When a marriage fails, all parties are wounded. Premarital and marital counseling is needed to cultivate strong marriages that stay together. A brief look at the communities where the marriage rate is low and the divorce rate is high will show visible signs that result from failed marriages. History shows that the strength of the nation directly corresponds to the strength of the family.

★ ★ ★

Young boys need to see husbands interacting with their wives using sacrificial love as their method of choice.

★ ★ ★

Staying married today is more challenging than it was in the past when there were fewer distractions. Many women and men today don't care if the man or woman they are interested in is married. We are noticing the growth of polygamy in many areas of the country. The mind-set of many Americans can be summed up in a commercial about Las Vegas: "What happens in Vegas . . . stays in Vegas."

Men need support staying married today more than ever before. Because the institution of marriage finds its origins in the church, it is only logical that the local church should make support available to men on a regular basis. This can easily be done by promoting annual or semiannual conferences. Your church can partner with organizations that specialize in promoting marriage and together encourage all married couples to participate.

5. Open a home for boys.

A tragedy is taking place right in front of our eyes. Little black boys are being adopted by gay male couples. This is tragic and violates anything closely related to common sense. Our response to this should be heat and moral indignation. The data shows that it is not in the best interest of boys to be placed in these settings. The reality is that they are being sacrificed on the altar of political correctness. With the myriad of laws that have been passed promoting this sordid practice, it is not going to get any better.

During their formative years, young boys need to see husbands interacting with their wives using sacrificial love as their method of choice. This is basic training for the next generation. Who best can fulfill this role in a young boy's life? I repeat: allowing gay men to adopt young boys violates anything closely related to common sense, and it ignores volumes of credible research that speaks against the practice.

We must provide alternatives for this scenario. One viable option is for us to adopt them ourselves. While I realize that adoption is not an option for all of us, it is viable for some. Another possibility is to open a home for boys. I know a man who did this, and he is willing to help others who are like-minded. A home for boys is a win-win situation for a church, because the government will pay for the home, and you can then serve young men while providing employment for a few members of the congregation. If you are interested in opening a home for boys, please contact us. We will put you in touch with those who can help you.

The church was, is, and always will be God's tool of choice to get things done in society. But a church that is not willing to adapt to the challenges of the new millennium will have a limited impact on future generations. We need to employ our very effective guerrilla-warfare weapon of prayer. In guerilla warfare you rarely see the enemy, but his attacks are lethal. Prayer is the most effectual weapon that the individual Christian or the church has. Let's begin to use it on behalf of our children as never before.

Consider doing something radical, something different. Although computers are challenging for some of us, the next generation is very comfortable with them. We must engage the young people in ministry decisions that affect them and get their perspective on technological issues. Be daring enough to stretch out and meet some needs that everybody sees. I promise you that it will bring excitement and new challenges to your congregation. There may be those that complain, but men of force can handle that.

★ ★ ★

Can I call you soldier?

★ ★ ★

ROLL CALL

☐ YES ☐ NO

1. Are you willing to be the one who takes new ideas to your church? Ask God to give you the heart of a soldier as you challenge the status quo regarding your church's ministry to young men.

☐ YES ☐ NO

2. Does your church have a men's class or a regular men's meeting?

☐ YES ☐ NO

3. Does your church minister to substance abusers? When a church I know of started a substance-abuse ministry, many members said, "We don't want them around us." What they did not already realize was that "they" were already around them—in their families, on their jobs, etc.

4. The author mentioned several benefits of starting a substance-abuse ministry. Which benefit do you feel could help your church the most?

☐ YES ☐ NO

5. Are your church and pastor progressive as they relate to these issues? If your pastor and church are innovative, thank them. Let them know you appreciate being part of a church that is meeting current pressing needs.

☐ YES ☐ NO

6. Does your church have a ministry to young men? Consider starting a ministry to young men, keeping in mind the fact that if you start it, you will be responsible for keeping it going.

☐ YES ☐ NO

7. Do you have a strong marriage? Do an intensive self-evaluation of your performance as a husband over the last year. Ask your wife what you can do to be a better husband. Listen to what she says, and then work on it. Marriage is a lifetime school that we never graduate from.

☐ YES ☐ NO

8. In your opinion, is opening a home for boys viable or even necessary?

☐ YES ☐ NO

9. Do you consider yourself a leader in your church? Our churches are in need of good leaders. If you determine to sacrificially serve your church, others will begin to follow, and you will then be in a position to make a difference. The key is always to lead by serving.

★ ★ ★

Men should be on the front line protecting America's children. Black men should be in the front of the front lines helping black boys. I have white friends who would lay down their lives for my children. BUT I would never let them beat me serving my children. No man should allow another man to serve and protect his children more aggressively than he does.

Dr. Harold D. Davis

★ ★ ★

CHAPTER EIGHT

WHITE MEN AND BLACK BOYS

When I was seventeen years old, I purchased my first house. I rented the house to a lady in the neighborhood, and when she paid the rent, I paid the house note. I did not know anything about buying a house, but my mentor and woodwinds teacher did. His name was Mel Gillispie, a white man who took an interest in me and freely shared his wisdom. I can give many accounts about how, during my formative years, a white man who saw potential in me assisted me in a significant way.

Principles Are Colorless

My father, John Davis, did an incredible job with his family. He modeled masculinity and taught his family wise principles that could carry us through life. He was the *man* in my life; but any wise father appreciates and is grateful for other like-minded men who invest in their son's life. As I have worked securing mentors for young men, I have encountered some interesting perspectives and strong opinions on the issue of who should mentor black boys.

In some circles, black men have a problem with white men who help black boys. I believe that all men should be on the front lines protecting America's children. But I also believe black men should be in the front of the front lines helping black boys. In fact, no man should allow another man to serve and protect his children more aggressively than he does.

Let the record show that my heart is warmed and I am grateful when I see white men mentoring, coaching, discipling, raising, protecting, and adopting young black boys. I think this is wonderful and the Christian thing to do. Yet, at the same time, the "black" man in me —the soldier, protector, provider, and guide—feels slighted. Please stay with me, because what I am about to say may sound contradictory and confusing if you don't read the whole chapter.

Healthy Racial Pride

When I was younger I used to experience strange feelings when I saw white men sharing principles with black boys. I did not understand why I experienced these strange feelings regarding my white brothers when I saw them on the front lines with black boys. Now that I have matured, I've begun to understand why I feel slighted when I see white men doing what black men should be doing. I realize that the feelings are natural and even healthy. Their origin is a healthy ego and family pride. It is a soldier's natural response to want to defend his own family, working in concert with other soldiers, while never idle when others do battle on his behalf.

★ ★ ★

When feelings of disappointment come, take your game up to the next level.

★ ★ ★

As a black man, when I see black boys in schools, I see sons, brothers, nephews, cousins, and neighbors. In other words, I think *family*. When they do well I am proud, and when they do poorly I am ashamed. When it seems that they are always the ones in detention or in the principal's or dean's office, I feel shame.

I repeat—black men who experience strange emotions when they see white men interacting with black boys are going through a *natural* series of emotions. But it is critical to understand and handle these feelings. For the benefit of the boys, the issue of black men feeling resentment when they see white men nurturing black boys needs to be understood by all parties. Learning how to sort out your feelings is a critical skill that men will employ for the rest of their lives as they experience assorted feelings that come with aging. If you learn to do it now, you will benefit for years to come.

Positive Energy from Negative Feelings

My method of dealing with the confusing and negative feelings is to become very active in the cause to help black boys. This high level of involvement helps me focus on positive results, not negative data. I would like to encourage all black men with the following advice: When feelings of disappointment come, take your game up to the next level. When you do this, you are no longer intimidated by what is not happening. Your masculine, fatherly need to raise the next generation is satisfied.

I still have mixed emotions at times when I see white men doing the job that black fathers, brothers, uncles, and cousins should be doing. Much of the frustration blacks feel toward whites at this point is frustration about what we are not getting done. It is not necessarily motivated by racial issues, but by disgust at the lack of leadership and involvement by black fathers. As I have matured, my desire has been to direct my frustration where it properly goes and not be guilty of misdirecting my anger.

Who Is My Brother?

What should the black man's attitude be toward white men who step up to the plate and help black youth? The only sane response for black men would be to say, "Thank you!" I praise God for the white men in my city who do this on their own and those who partner with me.

Over the years, I have personally recruited hundreds of white men to mentor both black and white boys. These men have had an incredible impact on future generations. I know of many young black men who would not be in college had it not been for the men who mentored them. I say *thank you* to those men. In this age when masculinity is under attack, I am very grateful for the strong soldiers who are standing on the wall meeting the need. "As iron sharpens iron, so one man sharpens another" (Proverbs 27:17 NIV).

Family Is As Family Does

Many years ago I made a discovery that changed my life. I discovered that Jesus was real, and everything He said was going to happen. I was simple enough to believe this and to respond appropriately. Shortly after I was saved I read 1 John 4:20: "If a man say, I love God, and hateth his brother, he is a liar: for he that loveth not his brother whom he hath seen, how can he love God whom he hath not seen?" That verse settled the issue of hating any man for any reason. I found in this verse a reason to distinguish brothers in the Lord from other men. Any man who presents himself to me as a brother in the Lord is afforded a special place in my heart, the place of brotherhood. We are family!

When we function in the Christian context of family, it makes the issue of racial culture a non-issue. We no longer classify ourselves based on racial culture but see our family members as those who belong to the kingdom where Christ is King. God distinguishes among three types of people:

- The Gentiles who trace their roots back to Adam who have not yet believed in Christ as Savior.
- The Jews who trace their roots back to Abraham who think a messiah is yet to come.
- The Christians who trace their roots and eternal life to Jesus Christ. These include Christians all over the world.

I realize that black or white is not the major concern, but Christian or non-Christian is the big issue. When a white man mentors a black boy, I see that man as a brother serving our Lord.

Our Response to White Brothers Who Mentor

1. See them as comrades in battle.

Certainly we are in a battle against a Devil with a new dress on. He has the same diabolical schemes, but he is now using new drugs, technology, radical feminism, the Internet, liberal schools, absent fathers, and many other contemporary tactics against young black men. We can no longer sit back and expect them to come to us on Sunday morning when they have so many things coming to them all week long. We need all of the help we can get from every available soldier!

2. Allow their involvement to challenge us to do more.

I am always challenged by God's soldiers, no matter who they are, and as a man I enjoy the challenge. A few years ago I was at a conference in Dallas, Texas. While walking down the hall in the hotel, Dennis Rainey, a white soldier whom I consider a friend, walked up to me, stuck his finger in my face, and almost yelled: "Don't Mess UP!" He then turned and walked away as if nothing happened. For a moment I was puzzled at this unprovoked challenge, but as I thought on what he said and considered his motivation for saying it, I was strengthened.

Many soldiers are turning in their armor and weapons for a life of ease. Other soldiers have sold their testimony for an adulterous affair with negative consequences that can impact eternity. Still other soldiers have embraced the Demas spirit of 2 Timothy 4:10 and forsaken God's kingdom because they love this present world and all that it offers more than the kingdom of God.

I realized a few years ago that I am going to die. After embracing that truth, I determined that since I am going to die, I might as well die with a sword in my hand fighting the Lord's battles. I am a better soldier because of those around me who also have their armor on and swords in their hands.

3. Seek to deal with any negative attitudes—surface or subliminal.

Some older black men have vivid memories of a time when we could not trust the majority of white people. I have asked God to help me get over that. You may have to do the same.

4. When we perceive that their motives are pure, thank them.

If I had the time, I would tell you about some incredible men who happened to be white. In retrospect, I know that God used them to get me to where I am today. I have a simplistic view of what influences people: some are used by God, and others are used by the Devil. When I sense the Spirit of the living God in a person, I thank them for their kindness while simultaneously thanking God for His grace in sending them to me.

5. Ask if there is anything that we can do to help.

I have worked with white individuals, churches, and organizations that needed insight into some nuance of black culture. Because they cared deeply and wanted to do a good job, I was glad to assist in any way I could.

Heeding the Battle Call

As I mentioned, I was made painfully aware of the need for aggressive, radical action when I found out that for every white male student suspended, there were seven black male students suspended.

I reflected briefly on how blacks responded to injustice in the sixties. I remember some people throwing bricks, protesting, and performing other militant acts. But then I asked myself: "How do you throw a brick at a statistic, at absentee fathers, at suspensions?" Those tactics were for another day, another era. In this new millennium we need a different approach.

As a soldier assigned to my city, I began to mobilize men in the schools to kick wisdom with young men. I soon realized that because of the absence of sufficient numbers of black men on the front lines helping black boys, all men were needed to step up to the plate and assist in getting the job done.

But at the same time, it only makes sense to me that black men should be rallying, organizing, and networking to address the crisis we see among our young men. I believe that as more black men take a good look at the negative downward trend of our young men, they will see the necessity of pulling out all the stops in meeting the need for fathers and father figures.

As I write these pages there seems to be an increase in the number of people who are speaking out on the issue of black adults taking responsibility for the condition of black youth. A few famous black leaders are taking up this cause. I am delighted to see this trend because it is long overdue. "If thou faint in the day of adversity, thy strength is small" (Proverbs 24:10).

★ ★ ★

Can I call you soldier?

★ ★ ★

ROLL CALL

☐ YES ☐ NO

1. Have you ever benefited from the wisdom of a man of another race?

2. According to the author, why do some black men experience mixed emotions when they see white men mentoring black boys?

3. What did the author say was his method of dealing with the confusing and negative feelings he felt?

☐ YES ☐ NO

4. The author speaks of the masculine, fatherly need to raise the next generation. Do you have that need?

☐ YES ☐ NO

5. Are you aware of the rate of suspension for black boys in your city? Acquire a copy of your local school's suspension statistics. Observe how the black boys are doing, and respond appropriately.

☐ YES ☐ NO

6. The author stated that he got busy in his city once he became aware of the negative trends. Do you embrace the title and responsibility of being called a soldier? Ask God to help you develop a sanctified soldier mentality.

☐ YES ☐ NO

7. Are your thoughts toward other races healthy?
Determine now to collaborate with other races to impact
endangered young black men. You may live in a difficult city,
but always remember that God has servants everywhere.

8. When you are challenged by a strong spiritual
man of another race, are you offended,
or do you see him as iron that is there to sharpen you?

☐ YES ☐ NO

9. Have you considered initiating a relationship with
a church that is racially different in order to recruit
additional soldiers to serve more young men?

☐ YES ☐ NO

10. The author became active in mentoring in 1995.
Have you had your awakening to the problem yet?

★ ★ ★

If we work upon marble,
it will perish; if we work upon
brass, time will efface it; if we
rear temples, they will crumble
into dust; but if we work upon
immortal minds and instill into
them just principles, we are then
engraving upon tablets which no
time will efface, but will brighten
and brighten all eternity.

DANIEL WEBSTER

★ ★ ★

CHAPTER NINE

LIVE SO THAT PEOPLE WILL FOLLOW YOU

I have learned through many years of marriage that if I simply set high standards when it comes to loving, serving, sharing, and giving, then my wife will reciprocate and do the same. By this I make myself the leader, and she becomes the follower. In other words, I do not have to demand to be followed and respected; it happens naturally because of my servant attitude. It is the servant who runs the house.

This system has worked well for me in most areas, although there is one area of my marriage where I simply demand to have my way—and that is holding the remote control. I have tried to share it and even allow my wife to hold it part of the time, but I just can't do it! It drives me crazy when she has the remote, and to my shame, I demand it back. You can see that I have some growing to do in the area of leadership.

Men are designed to be leaders. We are made with egos that must be fed. Our egos are designed to be fed primarily by our wives. When a man's woman esteems him, it helps him to take on the world. Our women are supposed to tell us that we are great and that we are their heroes. We are—and that usually helps us feel better. Our women and children are supposed to look to us for protection and provision.

When we meet the needs of our families, our ego needs are largely met.

One thesis of this book is that we need to have a following that is more substantial than our immediate family. Because of the "father voids" in our society, it is not difficult for quality men to develop a wide following. Playing the role of father, being a godfather, mentor, coach, counselor, and friend will all gain you a following. Many young people have told me that they want and need a father figure in their lives. Some of these young people were very astute academically, but had a hole in their heart that they were searching to fill.

★ ★ ★

Weak men talk about solving problems, but soldiers solve them.

★ ★ ★

It seems as though there are only a few men who understand the wonderful benefits received when you are available to the next generation. Actually, it is part of the maturing process. Men who allow their lives to flow into the next generation experience a quality of growth and maturity that other men do not experience. I believe that sacrificially serving the next generation is a critical element in a man's growth. Here are a few suggestions to help you expand the scope of your influence:

1. Be a man of integrity.

We have all met men who were men of few words, yet they were men of strength. These men have more people watching them than they would ever imagine. Their influence reaches further than anyone would realize.

I have learned something about men as a result of attending many funerals. A man's funeral is a powerful statement of the life he lived and the people he touched. Some men's funerals are very, very pitiful. They were men who lived for themselves and were not a lifeline to others. I remember several occasions when before the funeral we would have to hunt for people to carry the body from the hearse into the church. In worst-case scenarios, we would not have enough people to carry the body out of the church after the funeral. It is the culture of the military to give their fallen comrades well-attended funerals filled with pomp and pageantry. A soldier's last concern is who will handle their final arrangements.

I love what the Bible says about Stephen, the first martyr of the church. In Acts 8:2 it says, "And devout men carried Stephen to his burial, and made great lamentation over him." When Stephen died, men were lined up to carry his body to its final resting place. The verse describes the men as "devout." In other words, these were strong men of character, not just anybody off the street.

My brothers, you determine today—by your living and giving to others—who will carry you to your grave. Will strong men be lined up hoping for an opportunity to carry you out, or will they have to find some men off the street to carry your body?

2. Be a man of action.

My mother-in-law had two words she would say when she was challenged: "Watch me!" This is what she'd say when someone would doubt her word. My grandmother told me that talk is cheap. I have grown to realize that weak men talk about solving problems, but soldiers solve them. Too often there is a lot of dialogue about the condition of young black men but very little action. When a meeting or conference is held, powerful speakers encourage everyone, but often people leave the meeting the same way they came: uninvolved.

Talking without action builds a negative reputation. I have encountered many men who were proficient talkers but were weak in the doing department. I have noticed that many men who have spent time incarcerated are very good talkers. I believe they develop that skill while doing time. Unfortunately, once a man develops a reputation as a talker, he is soon marginalized by society and rendered ineffective.

I am always concerned with men who speak in the future tense. They say, "I am going to _______," or "Once I get _______, I am going to _____." It seems they are not doing anything right now, but always *about* to do something. These men love to get others involved in their dysfunction. They make comments such as, "As soon as my brother loans me his car, I'm going to get a job," or "The buses do not come to this part of town; what am I supposed to do?" Men like this find safety in the victim's seat, and the inaction of others on their behalf validates their failure.

A man of action will walk through snow to get a job. He sees obstacles as natural challenges to overcome, not someone picking on him. Our nation was forged by men of action, and our families must be sustained by men who understand this concept.

3. Be a lifelong student.

Life is constantly changing. The maturing process never ends, and to stay on top of things, you must be alert. Studying and learning is a skill that every man needs to perfect.

I recently became a grandfather. To be honest with you, I have really been trippin' about the whole thing. I don't feel old enough, smart enough, or rich enough to be a grandfather. Nevertheless, Junior is here! Oftentimes, life kicks you into the next phase with no preparation or consent from you. We should be lifelong students in the areas of self, marriage, and children. The shifting sands of time require that we make adjustments in these areas as the maturing process impacts us. Those who refuse to change are seen by others as inflexible, and life will move on without them.

As recently as yesterday I discovered an important aspect about my personality that needs to be adjusted. Most men stop adjusting at some point in their lives. That is when you are officially old. An ongoing self-study will keep you flexible and able to relate to the world around you. When you study yourself, you become more patient with the flaws of those around you.

4. Take advantage of your current season.

Life is a series of seasons. A man starts out as a boy who has to learn about life. He then becomes a young man who is strong but not very wise. During this period he should be under the authority of fathers, teachers, and mentors. Once he matures as a man, he takes a wife and raises a family. These are the productive wealth-building years, the years of strength and virility.

As the man grows older, his value to those around him takes a different form. He becomes valuable because he is "wisdom in residence" and provides a sense of stability. The tragedy is that this rich period is often ignored by society and undervalued by the man himself. I believe that we need to celebrate the wisdom that is available in our elders; and the elders need to stay active in sharing that wisdom.

Each season of a man's life can be rich if the right actions are taken. I suggest that you read up on this subject and be prepared to maximize your current season and help other men maximize theirs.

★ ★ ★

Can I call you soldier?

★ ★ ★

ROLL CALL

☐ YES ☐ NO

1. Tell the truth and shame the Devil.
Have you allowed your leadership qualities
to be squashed by others or die from lack of use?

☐ YES ☐ NO

2. Are you leading your wife or girlfriend by serving her?

☐ YES ☐ NO

3. Do you have a following that is more substantial than your immediate family? Get busy serving in your church and community. It has been said that if a man looks behind him and no one is following, it means that he is not leading but just taking a walk.

☐ YES ☐ NO

4. Do you have unquestionable integrity?
Determine to build your positive reputation.
Most Christians are gracious and will give you another chance.

☐ YES ☐ NO

5. If you died today, would your family have to pay pallbearers,
or would they have to turn people away?

☐ YES ☐ NO

6. Are you a student of self so you can make mature adjustments?

☐ YES ☐ NO

7. Are you maximizing your current season? Find an older man who has run the race well and very plainly ask him how he did it. Ask him how he got the strength to go on during trying times.

☐ YES ☐ NO

8. Have you made something happen that has benefited the people around you? Determine to be a man of action. Decide today that you will either make something happen or join others who are making something happen.

CHAPTER TEN

WHAT'S GOD GOT TO DO WITH IT?

The level of confusion about God and who or what He is has reached epidemic levels in America. A superficial look at our American history will show that it is saturated with people who believed in and trusted God. A casual look at history will reveal that the majority of the founding fathers of this nation depended on God. I could cite quotes from many of them, but allow these to suffice:

In 1793, George Washington wrote to John Armstrong:

> *I am sure that never was a people, who had more reason to acknowledge a Divine interposition in their affairs, than those of the United States; and I should be pained to believe that they have forgotten that agency, which was so often manifested during our Revolution, or that they failed to consider the omnipotence of that God who is alone able to protect them.*

And from President Abraham Lincoln:

> *I have been driven many times upon my knees by the overwhelming conviction that I had nowhere else to go. My own wisdom, and that of all about me, seemed insufficient for that day.*

Harvard University was founded in 1636 to train a literate clergy. Yale College was established in 1701, and the primary goal, as outlined by the founders, stated: "Every student shall consider the main end of his study to wit to know God in Jesus Christ and answerably to lead a godly, sober life."

George Washington Carver named his laboratory "God's Little Workshop" and never took any scientific textbooks into it. He merely asked God how to perform his experiments.

On June 14, 1954, the Congress of the United States of America approved "joint resolution 243" which added the words *Under God* to the Pledge of Allegiance.

With our rich Christian history accessible to all Americans, it amazes me that God is being systematically extracted from most aspects of civil society. You hear it in the news just as I do. It is progressing very rapidly across the nation to the point that we have a new generation of young people who do not know what Easter is about. As we observe the secularization of America, it would do us good to look at recent history to see what happens to a nation that extracts God from its daily life.

★ ★ ★

As we continue to extract God from the public sector, we will suffer consequences like the godless nations of history.

★ ★ ★

Joseph Stalin hated God and sought to extract Him from Russian society. Continuous persecution of the Russian Orthodox Church in the 1930s resulted in its near extinction. By 1939, active parishes numbered in the low hundreds, down from 54,000 in 1917. Many churches had been leveled, and tens of thousands of priests, monks, and nuns were dead or imprisoned. Stalin knew that once the church (the depository of truth) was out of the way, the people would believe anything. The nation declined very rapidly after this and has never fully recovered.

Hitler initially took a more subtle approach to conquering the church. He placed swastikas in churches next to the cross. In time he slowly removed the crosses and left the swastikas. Great men, like Dietrich Bonhoeffer, resisted Hitler's schemes at the cost of their lives. With the light of the church gone, Germany committed some of the world's greatest atrocities. They have not completely recovered from that loss.

Despite clear examples of the consequences of separating society from God, we are continuing full steam ahead in America to do just that. In my opinion, the problems we see with the family are a direct result of the godless attitudes that are becoming prominent in our nation.

Black People and Jesus

Of all the people in America who have a history with God, black people have certainly depended on Him. We are credited with creating spirituals and gospel music and a unique style of worshiping Jesus. Hundreds of songs speak of us crying out to Him in total dependence for deliverance. We as a people cannot afford to be like the children of Israel who turned from God who parted the Red Sea. Consider these lyrics from a slice of black history. The third verse of the Black National Anthem reads as follows:

God of our weary years, God of our silent tears
Thou who has brought us thus far on our way
Thou who has by thy might, led us into the light

Lead us forever in thy path we pray.
Lest our feet stray from the places, our God,
where we met Thee,
Lest our hearts, drunk with the wine of the world,
we forget Thee;
Shadowed beneath Thy hand, may we forever stand,
True to our God, true to our native land.

I have observed that the further a nation, city, people, or individual moves from God, the quicker the demise of that entity occurs. As a country, we would be foolish to believe that we can reject God and have a different outcome. As we continue to extract God from the public sector, we will suffer consequences like the godless nations of history.

Christ's Uniqueness

Among all the professed gods, Christ is unique. Consider the facts that Christianity is the only religion where:

1. God is represented as reaching out to man.

   "Behold, I stand at the door, and knock: if any man hear my voice, and open the door, I will come in to him, and will sup with him, and he with me." —Revelation 3:20

2. God pays the penalty for His subjects.

   "For God so loved the world, that he gave his only begotten Son, that whosoever believeth in him should not perish, but have everlasting life." —John 3:16

3. Heaven is guaranteed.

> *And hath raised us up together, and made us sit together in heavenly places in Christ Jesus.* —Ephesians 2:6

4. Hundreds of previous prophecies have come true.

One example is the birth of Christ.

> *Therefore the Lord himself shall give you a sign; Behold, a virgin shall conceive, and bear a son, and shall call his name Immanuel.*
>
> —Isaiah. 7:14

5. All scientific, mathematical, archeological, psychological, historical, physiological, and genealogical references in the Bible are 100 percent accurate.

For centuries, hundreds of skeptics from various fields such as law, medicine, science, mathematics, and literature have taken on the task of evaluating the Bible. Their sole purpose was to prove it false, only to discover that using the laws of hermeneutics (the science of interpreting literature) they could not disprove it. Many of these skeptics actually became believers.

> *All scripture is given by inspiration of God, and is profitable for doctrine, for reproof, for correction, for instruction in righteousness: That the man of God may be perfect, throughly furnished unto all good works.*
>
> —2 Timothy 3:16–17

Well . . . what does God have to do with it? Every man has to make that decision for himself. I like the decision that Joshua made when he said, "As for me and my house, we will serve the Lord" (Joshua 24:15). As the man, husband, and father, the decision you make will influence your family and possibly generations to come.

A good way to start with God is to erase everything you have ever known about Him and envision Jesus Christ facing you right now with His arms stretched out to you. This would be an accurate description of how Jesus views you. Jesus actually said, "Come to me, all ye that labour and are heavy laden, and I will give you rest" (Matthew 11:28).

God is about giving us rest—understanding and perspective and position—that relates to the madness we have to deal with every day. When I think about how difficult it is to understand the world apart from Jesus, it is easy to see why some people buy automatic rifles. They do it because they do not have God in their lives. A relationship with God gives a man peace and God's perspective on the many problems.

In reality, God has everything to do with it. He promises that if you seek Him, you will find Him. Consider the following Scripture promises:

> *All that the Father gives me will come to me, and whoever comes to me I will never drive away.* —John 6:37 NIV

> *If you confess with your mouth "Jesus is Lord" and believe in your heart that God raised him from the dead, you will be saved. For it is with your heart that you believe and are justified, and it is with your mouth that you confess and are saved.* —Romans 10:9–10 NIV

A common prayer that has been used by millions to become a Christian is, *Dear Jesus, I realize that I am a sinner; please forgive me of my sins and save me. Amen.* This is called a profession of faith. Professing that you believe in Jesus Christ is what is required to be saved. Growth, on the other hand, requires reading the Word, prayer, fellowship, older believers to help you, and time.

If you have made a profession of faith in Christ, seek out a Bible-believing and Bible-teaching church. It is critical that the church you join believes the following things:

1. The deity of Jesus Christ (He is 100 percent God)
2. The Godhead or Trinity (Father, Son, and Holy Ghost)
3. The inerrancy of the Bible (no errors in the original Scripture)

There are many issues that various Christian denominations may emphasize, but they are minor and would not stop me from worshiping with them. When a church has a problem with any of the items listed above, they are not biblical, and you place yourself in spiritual harm's way when you join them.

If you still need help and do not know where to turn, the best and safest advice I can give you is to contact the Billy Graham Evangelistic Association (BGEA). They have a rich history of leading millions of people to Christ. Their contact information is 1-877-2GRAHAM (1-877-247-2426). Another hotline you can call to talk to someone about Jesus is 1-800-NEED-HIM (1-800-633-3446).

Godspeed to you as you begin or continue your exciting journey in Christ. The old folks say that every day with Jesus is sweeter than the day before. I pray that this becomes your testimony. Joining God's army qualifies you as a soldier, but the question remains:

★ ★ ★

Can I call you soldier?

★ ★ ★

ROLL CALL

1. The Devil has some good stuff to keep you away from God. Remember that he will always bring the seemingly good stuff to keep you from the best stuff. Determine that you will work to develop the ability to distinguish God's best stuff from Satan's good stuff.

2. Sometimes God works like a microwave oven, and there are other times when He works like a Crock-Pot. Most often we get hungry before the spiritual meal in the Crock-Pot gets done and we settle for some spiritual fast food. God has promised to meet any man who would seek Him (Proverbs 8:17). Determine today that you will seek Him knowing that He will eventually respond to you in a manner you can understand.

3. When intellect is placed before God, He makes no sense. When the heart seeks God and finds Him, He satisfies the intellect with more than enough evidence to validate His existence. Millions of intellectuals have found faith in Christ and been satisfied. Determine today to fall in love with Christ and allow Him to stimulate you intellectually.

4. Some churches do a great job helping you feel God and a poor job of making you think. Other churches do a great job of making you think but do poorly at helping you feel God. Determine to balance your Christian life by fellowshiping with the larger body of Christ.

5. Congratulations on reading this book about men. What book have you decided to read next?

PIKESVILLE
1325 BEDFORD AVE
BALTIMORE, MD 21282-9998

12/14/2016 02:58:45 PM

Sales Receipt

Product Description	Sale Qty	Unit Price	Final Price
Forever® Postage	20	$.47	$9.40

Total: $9.40

Paid by:
VISA $9.40
Account #: XXXXXXXXXXXX6246
Approval #: 634260
Transaction #: 280
444502357305 5-99

SSK Transaction #: 54
USPS® # 230423-9555

Thanks.
It's a pleasure to serve you.

ALL SALES FINAL ON STAMPS AND POSTAGE.
REFUNDS FOR GUARANTEED SERVICES ONLY.

SUGGESTIONS TO HELP YOU GET INVOLVED

1. Seek to become sensitive to the needs of young men around you.

One way to do this is to look in the eyes of the young men you meet. Many of today's young men have limited eye contact with mature men. There is power, encouragement, correction, and many other benefits to be found in masculine eye-to-eye contact.

2. Reach back to your childhood and recall some of the things that frightened you.

Do this as a point of reference so that you can empathize with the fears of today's youth. The fears that terrorized you as a child are still active in the lives of today's young men. Your involvement in their lives can help chase those fears away.

3. Take the time to lovingly challenge a young man.

I was dropping my daughter off at her high school when I noticed a young man walking in front of my car with his pants drooping down. As he passed, I called him over to my car. (Note that we did not know each other.) I said to him, "Man I need for you to represent up in that school today. I need for you to make me look good." At this point he began to grin and I said to him, "You are a young black man, and you can make me look good when you take care of business at school." I then leaned over, bucked my eyes, and asked, "Are you going to take care of business today?" The boy stood up straight with a smile and said, "Yeah!" We then smiled at each other, and he left. Actions like this will help establish a sense of community again.

4. Support those who are already involved with young men.

Many soldiers have been engaged in this fight for some time. I wish I had the space to list every man I have met who is aggressively engaged in the battle to save young men. These men are my heroes. They saw the danger years ago and became engaged in the battle. If you want to get started, step up beside them, support, encourage, and learn from them.

5. Don't try to reinvent the wheel.

It is often difficult for men to support others. Get over it. Why go through all the trouble and expense to start something when others have already done it? Put your ego aside and copy or join what others are doing.

6. Start a Boy Scout troop.

My son is an Eagle Scout, and we can tell you from experience that when a young man has that on his résumé, it opens many doors for him. You may not know anything about scouting, but it is not difficult to learn. Go find a troop and volunteer.

7. Become an assistant coach on a local school team.

You may not know anything about sports, but you can be there as an example and for moral support.

8. Start a "men to boys" group in your church that meets once a week or once a month.

Use this meeting as a structure to do additional activities with the young men; share your collective wisdom.

9. Start a TALKS Mentoring Program in your city.

Lyman Rhodes III coordinates a program in Indianapolis where over three hundred children have benefited. Contact us for information on how to do it.

10. Develop the mind-set of a leader who leads by example and coordinates the efforts of others.

Giving and protecting is natural for a man. Unfortunately, our younger men are not cultivating that natural endowment. As a result, many of today's women and children unconsciously feel vulnerable and neglected.

11. Realize that life is unfair, and get over it.

Decide to use your influence to neutralize some aspects of life's challenges by providing opportunities for disadvantaged youth.

12. Go to church.

A study by Richard Freeman of Harvard University concluded that religion was the primary indicator in predicting a positive outcome for young black men. (Grandma knew this also.)

13. Love your wife openly.

Society needs to see this. Be sensitive and get and give some sugar in public. Take time to tell everybody how wonderful your wife is. If you do not feel that she is wonderful, begin to tell her that she is, and she will respond to your encouraging, kind words. Yes, she will.

14. Prepare yourself to dialogue with young men on the controversial issues of the day.

(Abortion, homosexuality, shackin' up, God, school, etc.) Don't guess about these things; just teach from the position of truth. Remember what the elders taught about these issues? The answers have not changed. You are now the oldest and must become the new fountain of wisdom for the younger generation.

15. Be committed to honesty and integrity.

There is nothing more powerful than a good reputation. On one occasion, an individual stole stationery from my wife's office and wrote an angry, ignorant, racist letter to the editor. Because newspapers like controversy, they printed it. We began to get weird phone calls informing us of the article. We were greatly troubled about this forgery. When I discussed it with an elderly person in the community, he told me not to worry about it, because our reputation could handle it. His response relieved me and reinforced the importance of having a good reputation.

16. Be very careful not to make mistakes that can ruin your reputation.

If you have blown it, begin to serve others consistently and realize that you may not be trusted for a period of time.

17. Let your tongue be an instrument of encouragement.

Develop the habit of always saying nice things about people.

18. Learn to save money.

If you are broke, determine to save as little as one dollar a week. It is not the amount of savings but the consistency that matters.

19. Embrace the fact that the most powerful thing you can do is give.
Giving starts a chain reaction that not only benefits the person you give to but also benefits you.

20. Become an advocate for one teacher or administrator.
Observe several and choose one who has a good heart and does good work. Begin to support them by speaking kindly about them to the students, and show up at key events to support their efforts.

21. Share with young men the mistakes that you have made and that you hope they do not duplicate.
Let them know how mistakes stay with you and hurt you for years to come.

22. Focus on foundational issues with young men, such as character, work ethic, and love for your brother.
Do not worry about their hairstyle, clothes, or music. If you keep interacting with them, you will get the opportunity to address these issues.

23. Address fatherhood issues whenever you get a chance.
Assume that society knows very little about this subject and repeat yourself often. It has been my experience that people are looking for guidance in this area. They will receive you if you speak with grace.

24. Write a letter of congratulations on your business letterhead to all young black men who excel academically.
If you do not have a business, provide the names and addresses of students, and ask a local business to do it.

25. Seek like-minded men to encourage you as you mature in your masculinity.
"As iron sharpens iron, so one man sharpens another" (Proverbs 27:17 NIV).

A FEW THINGS NOT TO DO

1. DO NOT get involved by yourself with a young boy and his young, lonely, good-looking single mother.
I do not have to expound on this point. Work through an organization, such as the men's group in your church, and allow the group to dialogue with the mother. You are not strong enough to do it alone.

2. DO NOT give money to kids without a positive lesson or work attached to the gift.

3. DO NOT engage in questionable activities such as letting a boy sleep at your house, taking overnight trips alone, or doing anything that can be twisted to harm your reputation.

4. DO NOT just observe and talk about the problem; GET BUSY!
On many occasions I have observed adults get together and talk about the problem. After the meeting was over, everybody went his or her own merry way, and no action was taken. The hour used to meet would have been better spent if each adult at the meeting had individually mentored a child for that time. Talk is not only cheap; it gives a false sense of accomplishment that often impedes real success.

This thesis statement is memorized by all boys who are enrolled in the TALKS Mentoring Program:

Every boy needs a man in his face,
challenging him with wisdom regarding
critical issues and decisions in his life.

EXPLANATION: Every boy needs a man who will firmly, unflinchingly, and lovingly correct him when he has made a bad decision. Our prisons are full of young men who had no one to get in their face, tell them that they were wrong, and then provide them with a solution.

—Dr. Harold D. Davis

There are at least one hundred additional chapters or subjects that could have been added to this book, but the goal of this book was not to address all the subjects related to masculinity but to ask one question:

★ ★ ★

"Can I call you soldier?"

★ ★ ★

WE SHALL OVERCOME

(New Millennium Version)

Sung to the traditional melody

We must save our boys

We must save our boys

We must save our boys today . . .

Deep in my heart, I do believe

We must save our boys today.

Christ will show us how

Christ will show us how

Christ will show us how today . . .

Deep in my heart, I do believe

We must save our boys today.

I will do my part

I will do my part

I will do my part today . . .

Deep in my heart, I do believe

We must save our boys today.

—Words by Dr. Harold D. Davis

A SOLDIER'S PRAYER

Lord, I pray to you because I can't comprehend
Why so many males refuse to be men.
Women and children are in need of support
Yet, many men have a self focus I sadly report.

Examples are lacking and there's a shortage of honor
I sense a refusal to put on the whole armor.
Where did black men lose it, where did we go wrong.
We must look to our fathers to place blame where it belongs.

A man should model masculinity and raise his own sons.
With absentee fathers the job is not getting done.
When life becomes distorted and sin is getting bolder,
Lord you ask the question: "Can I Call You Soldier?"

As you called Isaiah, you call us today.
Here I am, send me are the words we need to pray.
Soldiering this generation is a life well spent for God.
Help this Lord to be our goal as through this life we trod.

THE CHALLENGE

☐ YES ☐ NO

I accept the challenge to read this book and consider the principles contained therein.

☐ YES ☐ NO

I am willing to let my life be altered by truths I encounter in this book and beyond. I can consider my life in a nondefensive manner.

☐ YES ☐ NO

I understand that some principles are challenging, and as a man, I accept the challenge.

☐ YES ☐ NO

After reading this book, I may want to step up in certain areas of my life. Realizing the value of wisdom, I will seek out older wise men to help me.

☐ YES ☐ NO

I accept the fact that I have maturing to do. This book is the first of many steps that I intend to take to help me mature in my masculinity and develop my skills as a man.

☐ YES ☐ NO

I am excited to learn the skills necessary to fulfill my destiny as a man, husband, father, and community leader.

★ ★ ★

Signed this __________ day of ____________, 20____

____

Soldier in training

____

Witness

More from Lift Every Voice

THE TRAUMA ZONE:
***Trusting God for Emotional Healing*/**Dr. R. Dandridge Collins
Release Date: January 2007
ISBN 0-8024-8989-3
ISBN-13 978-0-8024-8989-0

This practical, encouraging, and biblically based manual will help trauma survivors—and their loved ones—move toward healing. Philadelphia-based, licensed psychologist Collins describes how trauma victims get caught in the trauma zone, a place they want to escape but can't. Some can't move forward, feeling stuck and victimized by their past. Some can't see, living in denial of what has happened. And others can't learn from the past, repeating the same mistakes over and over. All of them find they can't cope with the overwhelming emotions that accompany trauma. Dr. Collins believes there is a way out of the trauma zone and back to emotional health, a path he outlines in this practical, encouraging book.

TAKING CARE OF BUSINESS:
***Establishing a Financial Legacy for the African American Family*/** Lee Jenkins
ISBN 0-8024-4016-9
ISBN-13 978-0-8024-4016-7

Did you know the Bible contains over 2,350 verses dealing with money or possessions? Clearly God cares about the material side of life. In learning to apply God's standards to money and possessions, Lee Jenkins and his family achieved financial success and created a heritage of financial security to pass on to generations. You too can put these timeless, integrity-filled principles to work to build your house.

WHEN A MAN LOVES A WOMAN:
***God's Design for Relationships*/**James Ford, Jr.
ISBN 0-8024-6839-X
ISBN-13 978-0-8024-6839-0

"Everyone knows that Jacob of the Old Testament was a rascal, a usurper, a deceiver. But Jacob knew how to love a woman. If you want to know if a man really loves a woman, take a close look at what Jacob has to tell us." Pastor Ford takes a look at Jacob's lasting love for his wife, Rachel, gleaning insights on how men can meet the social, emotional and spiritual needs of their wives.

The Negro National Anthem

Lift every voice and sing
Till earth and heaven ring,
Ring with the harmonies of Liberty;
Let our rejoicing rise
High as the listening skies,
Let it resound loud as the rolling sea.
Sing a song full of the faith that the dark past has taught us,
Sing a song full of the hope that the present has brought us,
Facing the rising sun of our new day begun
Let us march on till victory is won.

LIFT EVERY VOICE

So begins the Black National Anthem, written by James Weldon Johnson in 1900. Lift Every Voice is the name of the joint imprint of The Institute for Black Family Development and Moody Publishers.

Our vision is to advance the cause of Christ through publishing African-American Christians who educate, edify, and disciple Christians in the church community through quality books written for African Americans.

Since 1988, the Institute for Black Family Development, a 501(c)(3) nonprofit Christian organization, has been providing training and technical assistance for churches and Christian organizations. The Institute for Black Family Development's goal is to become a premier trainer in leadership development, management, and strategic planning for pastors, ministers, volunteers, executives, and key staff members of churches and Christian organizations. To learn more about The Institute for Black Family Development, write us at:

The Institute for Black Family Development
15151 Faust
Detroit, MI 48223

We hope you enjoy this book from Moody Publishers. Our goal is to provide high-quality, thought-provoking books and products that connect truth to your real needs and challenges. For more information on other books and products written and produced from a biblical perspective, go to www.moodypublishers.com or write to:

Moody Publishers/LEV
820 N. LaSalle Boulevard
Chicago, IL 60610
www.moodypublishers.com